QUARKSA
THE BEGINNING

B. MARTINEZ

outskirts
press

TABLE OF CONTENTS

QUENOMOLY
(QUE-NOM-O-LEE)

Swirls of steam lofted from a lone cup of coffee sitting on a hot plate near the edge of his desk. Jim briefly sifted through emails from the night before. This was typically a pretty slow, quiet, and methodical job. He didn't mind. After all, he loved the cosmos. Ever since he got a telescope on his eighth birthday, he knew he wanted a career dealing with space in some fashion. However, many health issues prevented him from traveling in the distant heavens, so he made the best of his situation from his desk on Earth.

Jim's particular job description could be simplified by saying he watched space for anomalies. It could be meteors or comets freshly coming into the solar system or maybe ones that were already here and had a very regular orbit pattern. Although to most people, this might not be the most exciting job, he still loved it. He knew he was a bit quirkier than most, so it was a fitting role.

Unbeknownst to Jim, buried in a logged file longer

1

than a week ago was the only warning they would receive. If Jim didn't find it, Earth would be up for a rude awakening. He sifted through the data, but sometimes it was insurmountable, while honestly, most of the time, it didn't really matter if it was seen or not. If it was a real threat, it would show up again before it became an issue.

Unfortunately, Jim missed the most important signal of his career, not to mention his lifetime. Several weeks ago, two hundred and thirty million miles beyond Mars, a wormhole opened just long enough for a comet to traverse the plane. Although comets are notorious for leaving a bright tail trailing behind, this one was hidden, since it was in sync with Mars' orbit. Its tail was also irregularly short, considering how close it was to the sun. The comet was massive, yet the only time it was visible was when it first appeared through the white hole that brought it here.

In a matter of hours, the comet would meet Mars' far side and have an explosive impact. About that time, Gretta burst through the door.

"Jim, have you seen the images from the Mars rover?"

"What are you talking about, Gretta? You know my project has nothing to do with Martian activity. Besides, I just returned from vacation, and I'm two weeks behind," Jim answered with a matter-of-fact tone and an eye roll. He pushed his glasses up on his nose and returned to sorting through his unread emails.

"Of all the people to run and go see, why are you asking me?" he continued, as she stood staring at him with a look of disgust and frustration. Gretta leaned in to show Jim a picture from a Mars rover. The rover had been sending back streams of images of the terrain and the Martian sky.

"THIS!" Pointing to a picture she had snapped with her phone of an image from the rover, she shoved the camera closer to his face to make a point.

"It's an image from Mars! That is a comet, Jim! How could you miss it?" Gretta's anxiety and tension began to grow, which was evident from her voice and shaky hands. She waved her phone around, pointing to the picture.

"I sent a copy to your email, too," she remarked as if he were clueless.

"What?" Jim responded with a "give me a break" look on his face. He spun his chair around to view it on his computer that had a larger screen.

"This can't be accurate. I haven't seen any alerts yet," Jim said as his eyes filled with panic, clicking through various reports, emails, and instrumentation he used daily.

"I haven't been able to catch up yet since returning. I'm a couple weeks behind, but I should have got other alerts, and I never saw anything to even hint at a comet being so close. How did we miss it entering the solar system? It just can't be possible," Jim said, scouring through the data he was receiving from various devices. He checked multiple telescope readings and object identifier software that targeted space objects throughout the solar system.

"There it is," Jim said as he found the comet that was hidden behind Mars. But he had to find out how long they had until impact; they needed to know when it first arrived and the trajectory it was holding. He began quickly scanning backward to see where it came from. Then it disappeared when he reached nearly twelve days ago.

"It was only twelve days ago, Gretta. It literally came out of nowhere!" he said as he spoke to Gretta, who was standing next to his desk across the room.

"Uhuh…" she murmured flippantly, consumed in her phone. Jim shook his head with aggravation at her lack of interest. He pursed his lips and let out a sigh before moving to another telescope station to view the recorded history, verifying when the comet first appeared.

"Holy… did you see that? It was the comet's tail just before it went behind Mars," Jim said, playing the video back and forth, hoping to reveal details about how it got there.

"OH, MY…." His eyes widened, and he replayed the video to show Gretta.

"Look at this. Do you see that?" Jim asked, pointing to the monitor playing the video. Gretta made her way across the room to see what he was talking about.

"I don't see anything. What am I looking for?"

Gretta replied with a puzzled look, still a distance away from where Jim was sitting.

"It's not what you see. It's what you don't see. Watch! Look right here! I'll phase it back and forth," Jim said, pointing to a spot on the screen, then moved his mouse and typed away at the keyboard to get different angles, being sure to print as much as he could along the way. He zoomed in, then out, and all around where the comet first appeared.

"See right here? That group of stars, right there! Now they are gone. It has to be some sort of wormhole or spontaneous white hole or something," Jim said with excitement, but still fearful of what it meant.

"If my calculations are correct, we only have hours before impact on Mars. It's not going to be a direct hit, but most of it will," Jim said as he finalized the inputs into the trajectory systems.

"Great, there goes my rover," she said, rolling her eyes as if all her work had just gone up in smoke.

"We need to get the potential project outcomes to the division director. Let's go," Jim said, leading Gretta out the door. As they turned the corner heading down the hall, the hasty walk became a trot, pushing people out of the way. Jim dropped a few papers along the way, and Gretta scooped them up right behind him. Just as they got to their director's door, Jim burst in without so much as a knock.

"You have got to see this!" Jim exclaimed. And without hesitation, he threw all his paperwork on

5

Gerald Clumbly's desk.

"What is so important that you can't go through the proper procedure for documenting and reporting this?" Gerald asked, though not surprised by Jim's demeanor.

"This comet appears to have come through a white hole. It came out of nowhere just beyond Mars and is going to impact within a few hours!"

"Wait, what?" Gerald asked as he began to take notice.

"We have no time to delay! We have to be ready in case something beyond impact happens," Jim said with a frantic tone.

"OK, OK, we have to let the president know. I'll make the joint chiefs aware, so they can escalate it to the president. Get the team leads together and any other information you'll need, and meet me in the situation room," Gerald said calmly as he picked up the phone.

Within minutes, people began migrating toward the situation room with haste. Conversations started getting louder as the group tried to talk over one another. Conference lines and video calls also began to come online with lead officials. Nobody knew exactly what had happened or if the rumors they were hearing were true. Then Director Clumbly entered the room.

"Ladies and gentlemen… everyone… can I have your attention, please? We don't have a lot of time to cover this, and I'm not sure there's much else we can do at this moment anyway. About two weeks ago, a large comet began approaching Mars. It first appeared through what was thought to be a white hole. It went unnoticed for a fair amount of time because it was shielded from view behind Mars.

"As I said, we don't have a lot of time. Impact with Mars is imminent within the next thirty minutes. Momentarily we will be viewing the comet from one of Mars' rovers and the Hubble Space Telescope. After impact, telemetry teams will assess the situation to address our next steps."

The room was still quiet from the shock of the situation as the streams popped up on monitors around the room. Several different views and angles were available of Mars and the comet. They were all impressive and terrifying. Tension and anxiety were high, yet no one made a sound. There wasn't even time to notify public citizens yet, as they all watched with anticipation.

The United States wasn't aware yet, but three other countries' scientists noticed the comet simultaneously. They didn't have time to respond to the information either. It was unheard-of that the whole world had missed this potentially life-changing comet. And it had been the quietest two weeks, leading up to the largest cosmic event they would see in their lifetime.

They would all be watching different screens in the moments that followed, but the same event unfolded. Notably, most eyes were on the Mars rover, since it had the best angle and closest picture of the comet. It was also the largest on the main screen. A small countdown clock was in the top corner chipping away at the time left till Mars would forever be changed.

At this point, it was less than five minutes till the comet connected with the red planet. Anticipation increased as all eyes watched the clock near zero. A single camera on the rover was angled to view the sky and had an excellent picture, considering all the voyages it had been through. It was a clear picture of the Martian sky as a bright comet edged closer until it consumed the whole horizon.

Those who watched Hubble knew it would show the impact first, since it took about ten minutes to get signal feeds back from Mars. It also had the widest angle, giving a better scope of what was about to happen. Just as the time the clock reached zero, a large plume of smoke erupted from Mars' surface. It mimicked the action of a child throwing a rock into loose dirt, only there wasn't as much gravity to settle the soil afterward.

Gasps filled the room as they turned their eyes to the rover's camera. Shortly after, the rover camera went dark. It was relatively uneventful compared to the Hubble's view. Jim looked intensely at his laptop throughout the events, following his instruments and gathering as much data as possible.

"What are you seeing, Jim?" Gerald asked.

"It isn't good. Mars has left its normal orbit," Jim

said as Gerald's mouth opened in amazement. He wasn't expecting to hear it had moved the planet.

"It's drifting into a tighter orbit around the sun. There's a chance it will normalize with the new speed it's gained, but we won't know for a while," Jim begrudgingly conveyed.

"Wait... Mars didn't take the full impact! There's still a piece of the comet. It appears to have survived the collision, but its trajectory has changed. ...it's coming toward Earth," Jim said, as conversations in the room began getting louder again upon hearing the discouraging news.

Jim continued interpreting information as he computed it.

"It looks like it will make contact in about a week. The speed of the comet has significantly decreased. Let me do some final calculations, and I can get back to you in a few hours."

"Thank you, Jim. We will continue to update everyone as we get information. Until then, pray that this was the worst of it," the director said as he folded away his device and left the room.

It might have been three hours or so before Jim had the comet's remains' final trajectory and how it would strike Earth. Jim entered Director Clumbly's office and sat in a chair facing his desk.

"Well, what is it? What did you find?" Gerald asked while putting his face into his hands and rubbing his temples.

"Obviously, there's good news and bad news. There's no good way of giving the bad news. We have about five and a half days till it reaches Earth. The good news is we do have a chance, though," Jim said. Gerald let out a sigh as he gave a noticeably long blink.

"And... how do we utilize this 'chance'?"

"It is too big to bounce off the atmosphere, but it is coming in somewhat flat. It's possible if we could create a blast large enough, it could shatter the fragments and burn up in the atmosphere. Or it could stay intact and bounce off instead of continuing through to hit Earth."

"Obviously, we need to take action either way, to ensure humanity's survival. Do you see any problems with using nukes?" Gerald asked.

"The largest issue is that we need a lower altitude to make the largest explosion possible, ensuring its effectiveness. If the detonation is too high, it won't have enough oxygen and won't be effective. Even if the rocket were carrying extra oxygen, it wouldn't explode with the same force at that altitude," Jim said pursing his lips together, making an "I don't know what else to do" look on his face, and shrugging his shoulders.

Gerald looked up.

"Thanks for your help, Jim. I'll escalate the information. Let me know if you come across any further information." With that, Gerald picked up the phone and made a few calls to chiefs of staff and others who could let the president know.

Less than twenty-four hours later, a meeting was scheduled with the same group who watched the Mars impact. The only difference was that the president wanted direct information this time. Many heads of the departments continued to present the knowledge they had gained through the course of the events. While everyone was receptive, it was sometimes difficult to grasp the severity of the possibilities. All the information was based on information Gerald's team had provided.

"Our only option is a Hail Mary. Our best hope is to throw as much tactical power at it as possible and pray for the best, but it still needs to have perfect timing," Gerald said.

"Are you suggesting launching coordinated nukes?" Madam President asked with a condescending tone.

"Yes, and it will have to be a global effort, but it will also need an extra payload of oxygen," replied Gerald.

"It is the only way we can generate enough force to push it away or completely destroy it. We have less than four days before we will need to launch," he said.

"Mr. Clumbly, coordinate with my staff to continue forward with launch coordinates. I will provide the launch codes when needed. I will also contact other world leaders who are equipped and capable of donating their weapons for the greater good," the president said and promptly disconnected the meeting.

A few days later, a rural store clerk was sitting

behind the register reading his newspaper. The wind blew dust across the well-packed gravel road when a truck came skidding up to the gas pump as the gentleman behind the counter looked up, averting his eyes from the callous daily news.

Shortly after, several other vehicles made quick stops near the pumps, sending dust clouds in all directions, covering the vacant cars sitting in the parking lot.

"What in tarnation?" he muttered to himself as he folded the paper, placing it on a shelf under the counter.

The man from the first vehicle finished filling his tank. He jogged through the door, sending the bell hanging above the door violently clanging in all directions. He quickly scanned the area inside the door and found an empty cart.

"Careful there, buddy, this is a family business!" the man behind the counter hollered as the man whisked the cart toward the back of the store. The clerk seemed puzzled as he heard the man filling the cart loudly with items he found useful. After filling the cart, the man hurriedly continued to the front of the store, occasionally bumping into racks and the counter on the way.

"What's got ya flustered, son? And why do you need all those supplies? Three packages of toilet paper? There hasn't been a pandemic in years," the clerk said, looking strangely at the man pushing the cart as his drawl became more evident.

"Haven't you heard the news or been outside? There's a comet chunk that's going to hit Earth! The city stores are already sold out and have bare shelves. I'm heading up to my cabin near the mountains," the man said, speaking relatively fast.

"Alright, I guess you have to do what you have to do. That'll be two hundred eighty-three dollars and fifty-two cents."

"Aren't you worried about staying here?" the man questioned as he swiped his credit card for his groceries and gas.

"Son, if the good Lord decides to bring me home, I can't stop him. Be careful out there."

The traveler loaded up his vehicle and sped away, tossing dust and gravel on the other people filling up with gas. The world had no idea what to expect. Leaders reassured populations that it wouldn't be an issue, but lies only go so far, even ones meant to protect the people.

World leaders and elites had begun quietly hunkering down in their safety zones, leaving the rest of the population to fend for themselves. Although general public concern was low on the radar, the government was sure to provide safety to many experts in various fields that would be essential after the catastrophic event. All over the world, they took refuge in bunkers deep within the earth, shielding them from debris and fallout in the worst-case scenario.

Many world leaders wouldn't even give locations of

potential impact for fear of mass panic and subsequent deaths resulting from the alarm. Even the President of the United States refrained from speaking or sharing information with the public. It seemed to be at a time when self-preservation was at a peak, and caring and empathy struggled to survive.

In the final seconds before launch, the codes were read, and the missiles were armed. From all over the world—the United States, Russia, China, United Kingdom, and France—rockets were launched to prevent the comet from reaching the Earth's surface. The enormous payload the missiles carried was nothing short of amazing. There had never been a coordinated event this large to save humanity. It would be evident soon whether it was a heroic feat or a horrible disaster.

Rockets converged on the spot that was calculated to have the most effect. One misfire or miscalculation could be cause for even more alarm. At that point in time, one rocket's timer that was incorrectly coded, exploded.

It wasn't immediately known which country had sent the missile. Still, that singular premature explosion lit the sky much earlier than intended. It caused a chain reaction and the whole cluster detonated before reaching its target. The flash was brighter than the sun. Although the comet was close enough to be destroyed, there would be no going back to normal. Ice and fragments instantly disintegrated, while part of its core melted and created an aerosol effect that wasn't anticipated.

Following the bright flash, plumes of mysterious dark clouds began to shadow Earth. The dark smoke multiplied when it entered the jet streams and other cloud structures as it began to spread worldwide, consuming any light that dared shine through to the Earth's surface. It completely blocked out the sun and any vision into space. A heavy night fell on the third planet. It would be weeks before it finally dissipated, leaving a hazy green atmosphere that would last for centuries.

"I've done everything I could. I escalated the information like I was supposed to, came up with a great plan that could save the planet. I covered every angle I could think of to help survive the comet. Still... they couldn't even take me with them to their shelters. I'll show them. I'm going to find out exactly what happened if it's the last thing I do," Jim said with hurt and frustration.

The days after the Quenomoly, Jim came and went to his office, like regular, choking in the mysterious fog that engulfed the planet. As days turned into weeks, fewer and fewer people showed up for work. They were getting sick and staying home or sheltering somewhere out of sight. Jim continued his daily ritual of making his coffee and sitting at his lonely desk sifting through the data that was left from the event. He kept thinking that if he could understand what happened, maybe it would help someone fix it.

He sat coughing at his computer, replaying the footage of when the comet appeared. He noticed there were different sounds from the white hole that didn't match other recorded white holes. The sound was different and a mixture of many different things happening in space, almost like a man-made anomaly.

Jim hurried and began diving deeper into his work, not noticing he was coughing harder and harder as droplets of blood and saliva speckled his monitor. His breathing became more laborious, and he began to feel his lungs swell, preventing him from breathing. Gasping for air, still coughing blood on the monitor and keyboard, he finally saw it. It was a tiny shadow lingering behind the large comet.

Shakily, he zoomed in with the keyboard. Jim reached in front of him, smearing blood across the surface of the monitor, where he saw the strange saucer-like image as he took his last gurgling gasp. His lung and heart grew weary of the battle between the shrinking space in his chest. After a brief thrash, he plunged into the keyboard.

ATYPICAL DAY

Several centuries later, it was a late Friday evening when Zillah pondered just how much the world had adapted to so many unforeseen circumstances over the years. She was sitting in her office on this warm summer night as the onset of darkness began to fall. Zillah hesitated when she caught the surreal twilight of the orange sun. An all too familiar hue of green engulfed the sub-stratosphere, shunning the distant source into the night.

Most people around Zillah wondered how they would cope in the years to come and what their future would hold, but Zillah only found herself observing the past. Merely two months earlier, she had turned fifty-four. What was a lifetime to her under the green and orange skyline was only a small nugget in the world's evolution. Although it seemed millennia ago, she could still remember her sixteenth birthday.

Zillah was home studying advanced courses with her mom. She was homeschooled and advanced very quickly through the material, even though sometimes she got bored. As she finished a class on astrology and the cosmos, her dad walked through the door from a hard day in construction. Guillermo's job was well paid but very dangerous, since it was mostly outdoors and exposed to toxic elements all day.

He set his large helmet down on the table and then rested a small gift box beside it with a greeting card balanced on top. Zillah opened the envelope to find a card that read "My most beautiful daughter, I love you more than anything and cherish what time I get to spend with you. You are God's blessing to me, here and beyond. Happy Sixteenth Birthday, Dad."

Then she opened the box resting beside the helmet and found a bracelet with assorted space and scientific symbols and sayings on them. There was only one different charm amongst them that said, "I love you to Mars and back." She eventually had it converted into a necklace after he passed. She wanted to keep his memory close wherever she went. She often found herself digging out old news stories, not necessarily because she wanted to, but because her job required it.

"I still can't believe they actually used these things," Zillah commented as she carefully put the Blu-ray in the antiquated player.

A distant voice called, "I agree, but at least the computers evolved from being the size of a whole room."

It was Garret Blevins, Zillah's lab assistant and long-time friend for the past twenty years. They met when Zander Enterprises first began to construct the Quarksandrium project. As Zillah watched and listened to the historical pictures and news cases that accompanied them, "The Minnesota I-35 bridge collapse is not suspected to be a terrorist attack...."

"Hey Zillah, did you have disk 09-66-11-2001 out for review? It's not in the archive sleeve," Garret interrupted from the adjoining lab station.

"No, I haven't seen it. Did you look in the third viewing station?" Zillah replied.

"You were right again, just like usual. Have we found anything recently that's changed?" Garret inquired.

Moments passed and Zillah responded, "We haven't found anything, and we're just about through the burn period. Everything looks the same."

"Alright, Dr. Z. I'm going to head home for the evening. It's already seven," Garret said as he let out a noticeable yawn.

"OK, Garret, see you next week."

Zillah often worked late searching for solutions in hopes of someday finding the answers she was looking for. She went to the last disk, which would be the deciding factor if anything significant had changed from their recent excursions, "The Quenomoly." It was a particular disk often referenced because it was the end of the period they always surveilled. Throughout their missions, everything remained the same.

The Quenomoly was a well-documented event in the twenty-first century. It was thought that it was first called this because comets are white, like a cue ball. Although nobody really understood why it was spelled with a Q. The anomaly also collided with Mars, much like a pool ball, sending it into a new orbit considerably closer to Earth. It turned out to be a lousy year for billiard puns.

At nearly nine, and the phone rang. Zillah's daughter, Eirwen, called from the hospital, letting her know her husband was awake. It wasn't often that Jorge would be fully awake in recent months. Zillah hurriedly put on her exosuit and walked with purpose down the halls. The lab that she worked in was run by a company that was contracted by the government. This particular lab was the only one of its kind; it housed many projects dealing with time and space, such as hers.

The Parlin Center was appropriately named after the first town they ventured to in the Quarksandrium project. The facility was more than just an assortment of government bids, especially for Zillah. After all, it was her building design that gave its uniqueness. The interior looked like any other high-tech building of the time, but the building's layout made it stand out from the others. The building resembled an intricate crop circle when viewed from above, which became well known in previous centuries.

The interior of the building was made up of multiple sections that moved annually, creating new patterns. It had been built nearly ten years ago, but the room configurations would never repeat for the next sixty years. It was almost impossible to find your way through this building without an updated map. Some workers would consult the navigation guide built in their suit while others wore heads up display within their eyewear. It was essential for Zillah's office to be in the building's center to grant her quick access to the most necessary rooms and storage of the project.

As Zillah neared the doors leading outside, she finished putting on her exosuit. She pressed the button sequence on the suit's forearm, and the helmet assembled around her head to seal the apparatus. Anyone venturing outside wore an exosuit because of the harsh environment and damage it would inflict on the human body. It has been over two hundred years since the Quenomoly tarnished the atmosphere. It didn't take long after the event for people to realize that unfiltered air caused diseases and infections that couldn't be cured. Humans had little resistance to all the new microbes that evolved during the burn period. Once the infection took root, death was inevitable.

There were many kinds of suits that differed in color and function. Military units typically dressed in a range of camouflage-colored skins, mercenaries sported black, and civilians most often wore white. Even though all uniforms protected people from being in the unfiltered air, military, mercenary, and other suits had enhanced abilities and customized enhancements for their job role. Zillah's suit was partially blue. Other parts were white and had markings of scientific significance to reiterate she was a scientist. Her name-plate, "RUTHVEN," was scribed in gold lettering above her right breastplate. It was notable that the standard government suit was colored to match the division a person was assigned.

Most government and research facilities workers walked to where they needed to go in the year 2329. Extravagant transportation was forbidden within most sectors, although there were exceptions to every rule.

There were many discoveries over the years. Power sources were no longer an issue like they were hundreds of years ago. Fossil fuels, solar, and wind energy are of historical relevance, but the Quenomoly brought new alternatives to power and transportation. In fact, previous generations may view these technological advances as almost alien-like in design.

Many setbacks and tragedies resulted from the Quenomoly. Still, humans had many accomplishments and breakthroughs that wouldn't have otherwise been accomplished except through the catastrophe. Some may have been discovered by accident; some were just invented by people with strong visions.

Several decades after the event, scientists found that the microbes left in the atmosphere contained energy that wasn't present before. When developing new power sources, scientists used bacteria from the fallout in their experiments. Molecules were collected from the tarnished air and mixed with a solution, harnessing its energy. Over the years, the natural progression adapted to many types of personal transportation machines, hover crafts, powered boards, flying vehicles, and space exploration ships.

After discovering that cellular power could be produced from environmental toxins, mankind began filtering the atmosphere, literally fueling their economy. It was initially thought the air would eventually return to normal if they continually removed the rogue debris. Unfortunately, the invading particulate had a different agenda, and much like in a petri dish, the alien microbes multiplied. Even with filtering, the terminal density never changed once it was disbursed and stabilized throughout the atmosphere.

It usually took Zillah about twenty minutes to walk her route to the hospital, providing she didn't stop along the way for a snack. The hospital's lobby area she often entered through didn't have much traffic. Generally, just one person was stationed at the desk near the elevator.

Zillah paused before approaching the hospital's entrance to marvel at the seven large cylinders along the building's front. As she walked through the fourth carousel-like revolving door, tarnished air was exchanged with fresh air. This was typical of most large buildings to keep the contaminated air outside in an efficient manner.

"Good evening Miryam," she waved as she passed by the small information desk.

"Hi, Zillah, nice to see you. Have a wonderful visit."

Zillah stepped up to the elevator doors and touched her visitor badge to the scan plate calling the lift. Soon, the doors opened, and she stepped inside. Technology and security enhancements had indeed changed over the years. Gone were the days of manual labor of pressing buttons, biometrics, and badges almost guided a person where they were supposed to go. Sometimes it was rather creepy.

As the elevator lifted her to the sixth floor, Zillah took a minute to catch her breath from her brisk walk. When the doors opened, she noticed the drab blue and grey colors on the sixth floor. Unlike the others that were bright and cheery, the sixth floor was different for some reason. She often wondered why they left this floor so drab. She paused and let out an exhausted sigh of defeat as she answered her own thoughts with the typical response lined with disgust and a touch of anger as she shook her head. *Why would they brighten it up? Everyone here is going to die anyway... So what does it matter?* She was almost to her husband's room when she met Eirwen and gave her a hug.

"Everything OK?" She asked her daughter.

"Yeah, dad hasn't really gotten any better, but he's doing OK and asking for you. I've been pretty busy getting everything ready for the wedding next year. I really would like dad to be there," Eirwen said as Zillah looked sadly at her and gave her a tighter embrace than before.

"I'm sure everything will work out for the best,

Eirwen. We both love you very much," she said as she looked at her daughter holding her hand.

Zillah's research doesn't directly deal with the diseases that plague the Earth. Still, if she succeeds, it could make a significant change to the atmosphere providing a chance for a stable environment for humans again. Since Jorge had been infected, it made her quest to find answers all the more critical, especially in the last decade.

Zillah has been working on the Quarksandrium project for approximately twenty years. But it was only in the last ten years that they have made surmountable progress. Her desire to find a solution initially started when she was a young woman after her father, Guillermo, died from one of the diseases the Quenomoly created. He was cleaning an exhaust fan at the construction site when his exosuit filter failed, causing him to inhale tarnished air.

As she grew older, she found herself studying more and more in the field of science. She often wondered how she could fix the air problems so people wouldn't die when exposed to the unfiltered air. Zillah had no idea what was in store for her or how fate would play a significant role in the years that followed.

Shortly after she began the building phase of the Quarksandrium project, she met Jorge. She quickly fell in love with everything about him. It was easy for anyone to see that their chemistry was unique, and they were designed to be together. It wasn't a surprise when Zillah became pregnant several months after the project's build started. Shortly after, they decided to get married. She was heartbroken when Jorge contracted the disease nearly nine years later. She knew it wasn't her fault, but why had people in history been so careless?

Since Zillah's quest required her to look through history meticulously, she was constantly reminded of the tragic event that caused all this destruction. The Quenomoly could only have been avoided by the technology they didn't possess at the time. Shortly after the second consecutive monumental president change before the event, anarchists, extremists, and other groups attacked common targets. Terrorism became less isolated as the next few years went by and began reaching further around the globe.

The event would be the only chance of bringing humanity back together. Yet, still in the face of extinction, activists managed to compromise missiles in foreign countries, loading them with bioweapons. Socialistic reforms were instituted through elements of progressive law. They gradually chipped away at the true independence of what was called the free world.

Often claims were that of 'protecting' the people. However, no amount of cyber spying or truth squelching would enlighten them that they were minutes away from catastrophe. A large space rock of unknown contents, combined with nuclear material and many bio-contaminants, caused the world to turn dark, releasing

QUARKSANDRIUM: THE BEGINNING

unprecedented amounts of toxins.

It was the last anyone would see of the rockets red glare. The skyline was tarnished forever, leaving a green hue through future generations. It caused widespread infection and disease, but the worst of them was called Epsiletacell disease. In the years that followed, anyone who wanted to live or move on public transportation took a government vaccine and a tracker. Paranoia continued through the burn period by leaders only seeking their own agendas, hungry for power under the guise of safety.

Common disease attributes were found in most of the viruses and illnesses created by the Quenomoly. It is thought to be the root cause of other infections. After infecting its host, it slowly metastasizes, causing a long, painful death. Even so, the human body is remarkably resilient over time. Although future generations may eventually be immune, it would take thousands of years to adapt and mutate, benefiting both the bacteria and the host. As with any disease or illness, medical discoveries evolve, allowing us to prolong death for a short while.

Zillah and Eirwen walked the short distance to where Jorge's room has been the past three years. Although he had various health issues since the incident nine years ago, the last three have been the worst. Early after the infection, his body was more durable, and he recovered quickly without knowing what was wrong. As the years faded, so did his health, along with the speed of his recovery. Hospital visits became more frequent, and overnight stays became normal.

Zillah brushed her fingers across the numbers of the room, thirteen. Sometimes the feel of material and different textures under her fingers gave her a sense of belonging. Sometimes it may have appeared to be a nervous tick, but it was mostly just to feel like she had a purpose. Maybe it was fate that he was in such an unlucky room number, or perhaps it was meant to be a new beginning. Either way, she knew there was nothing she could do to change the situation.

"Hey, sweetie, how are you doing today?"

Zillah asked Jorge with a slight grimace on her face that accompanied her empathy. Jorge gathered the strength to talk,

"Zillah…My Love… I remember the day I walked into the… Quarksandrium project…you… were so beautiful…"

It was difficult for him to speak since the disease spread to his lungs. He often had to take breaths and muster the strength to get the words out he wanted to say.

"Zillah, I love you… it won't be long… I just want… you to know… you…are still just as beautiful… and I will always love you."

Jorge held Zillah's hand as he relaxed again and drifted back to sleep. Zillah sat in the chair near her husband's bed while she grabbed his hand. As she wiped the tears away, she began to think about the events that led up to her husband's infection.

Eirwen paused a moment before pulling her mother's attention away from her dying husband.

"Ok, now that he's resting, back to what I was saying. Do you have time next week that we could go over some of the plans for the wedding?" Eirwen questioned from a chair across the room. Zillah haphazardly answered and continued the conversation as Eirwen was clearly focused on her own needs instead of her father's well-being.

Zillah continued holding Jorge's hand and began reminiscing as she gave minimal effort to Eirwen's questions about the wedding. The hollow conversation continued with Eirwen while Zillah's mind separated her thoughts and focused on Jorge and their previous life.

FLASHBACK

Throughout the years, Zillah and her team have had many breakthroughs and advancements with the Quarksandrium project. It was ten years ago that they had the most considerable breakthrough. The Quarksandrium was nearly finished; it only lacked a few minor tweaks to come to life. Almost two decades of Zillah's work was about to take another significant step toward the ultimate goals she wanted to achieve.

In the early days of the Quarksandrium, the machine and its computers were large and bulky. The machine's focal point was a sizeable octagon-shaped metal frame that used ten-inch- thick square tubing, surrounding its edges, and spanning twelve feet. Various colored wires connected the machine's components to power sources. At the same time, others ran to sensors and computers to document every detail. Many even had a redundant set of connections in case the first failed. A bundle of hoses ran across the back of the unit, connecting the portal with various cooling systems that supplied both air and liquid agents to keep the proper temperature.

"Jorge, could you hold the gyroscope while I check the focal point?" Zillah asked.

"Sure, just let me finish resealing these two wires," Jorge replied.

Jorge completed his task along the edge of the frame, then held the center of the unit to keep it from moving so Zillah could remove several of the triangle-shaped faces from the polyhedron. The center's orb had twenty sides and spanned about four feet.

Inside the polyhedron were various circuit boards and wires with a cavernous center. The front of the machine was angled slightly upward toward the ceiling. Wires, cables, and hoses gathered behind the machine, then ran the room's length to where the servers and network equipment were positioned on the opposite side.

"Garret, would you mind handing me those spare jumper wires laying on the console over there? It appears this is a three-person job instead of just one," Zillah said, holding the large orb still while contorting her body in a strange yoga-like pose.

"Sure, be right there," Garret replied.

Before the frame was updated years later, bundles of wires and hoses weren't organized very well. They caused havoc for anyone trying to maneuver around the platform. The multitude of cables and hoses used for cooling, fine-tuning settings, and feedback from many sensors gave more data than would ever be needed. It might have looked like a bunch of junk through the eyes of a bystander, but it was an absolute miracle to the team.

It seemed like any other day in the lab with Zillah checked the diagrams against the physical connections of the Quarksandrium. All the connection points met her approval. They were ready to flip the switches and make it light up. The scientists gradually returned to the control room and went down the standard power-on checklist, calling out each step as they turned the machine on.

"Bring up the primary instruments…" Zillah called with a hint of a funny accent, maybe from something she had heard in the past or a movie. Jorge and Garret briefly looked at each other and shook their heads before Jorge piped in with his best impersonation.

"I'm giving it all the particles I've got, Captain," Jorge said with a failing Scottish accent as Garret tried to hold his laughter.

They quickly began pushing power buttons on the monitors and various computers along the command center. The computers lit up one by one, beginning their boot sequence. Several of the units provided calculations and visual alerts on the large transparent screen between the Quarksandrium and its users in the control room. The screen was unique in that it showed individualized data to each of its users.

The Quarksandrium was clearly visible from all

angles of the control room through these informational displays. However, the position of each chair would dictate which notifications were shown to each commander. Many secondary systems that required less attention were lined around the back of the control room using older equipment. If data was gathered or input into the Quarksandrium, you would see it replicated on one of its screens.

"Ravyn, when this row of equipment gets turned on, always initiate from the door of the control room toward the inside wall," Zillah said, instructing the new intern as she made quick work of powering on the ancillary workstations along the room's wall opposite the Quarksandrium. The monitors flashed and flickered as the computers went through their cycles. Quickly, they all began to come online and go to a ready state.

"Who do you want me to shadow during this event, ma'am?" Ravyn questioned.

"We only use the term 'shadow' to refer to a past time continuum, but follow my lead. You'll do fine," Zillah advised her.

Most of the time, it was only the three who worked on the project. Although some days, they may have had an intern help with less significant operations. Many interns rotated through projects in different departments throughout their onboarding process within the company.

Today the intern, Ravyn, was with them in the control room. She had been hoping to land a permanent spot with the team. It wasn't long ago that she lost her mother to one of the diseases spawned from the Quenomoly, as many people had over the years. Since working at Zander Enterprises was a coveted environment, the intern list was long and challenging to make.

Once selected to be an intern, most would stay with the company their entire career. Tasks given to interns were usually trivial and didn't require in-depth knowledge of the project. Still, if the fit was right, the department usually requested that they stay longer.

Zillah returned to her cockpit chair in the middle and slid closer to the controls. She pressed the last power buttons on the computers they would need to command the portal.

This operational series of machines, lined across the observation windows, usually required at least three technicians to monitor and operate. They were located in the central control room, which Jorge, Garret, and Zillah commanded.

Zillah was in the center seat. She could see the whole Quarksandrium with the essential elements highlighted that she needed to monitor. Most of these elements were related to navigation, which included time and location. The logistics were mind-numbing to most people. It took her years to understand the nuances and quirks of how the equipment was assembled.

"Temperatures are optimal and ready for initialization," Jorge called as he touched virtual buttons on his panel, releasing gas at various points of the machine. White clouds of gas shot out as he released the tension on the lines to keep the temperature within the correct range. Jorge was on Zillah's right side. Many of the sequences were automated, but he could fine-tune power, atmosphere, and portal temperatures as needed. His view of the device allowed him to see data related to any aspect of the portal's power, temperatures, and other critical alerts.

"Core integrity is at one hundred percent. All the readings look great," Garret followed Jorge's introduction. As the mission began to delve deeper, the crew became more serious and dropped the accents. To Zillah's left, Garrett operated the last station. Garrett oversaw the mechanical aspects and stability of the Quarksandrium. He loved to swipe through the various notification screens, viewing sensors and minor alerts to keep the machine running optimally. Sometimes he might help Jorge with changing power values to optimize the load of the device.

The remaining duties were split among the three scientists. It was similar to pilots flying a large plane. They each knew how to operate the whole machine but mostly focused on their own portion of responsibilities.

"...verify sensor conditions..." Zillah was on a roll with her accent as it began to get a little thicker. Sometimes she went too far, though, and ran a good joke right into the ground.

Garrett rolled his eyes, shook his head again,

and smirked as he scanned across the monitors. He watched the translucent screens as the black squares changed to green circles and switched to a ready state. A variety of colors indicated which sensors had come online or had issues. Those that were still in transition were displayed across the room. Everything was going well, till a vibration started from one of the cooling fans.

"Where's that noise coming from?" Zillah asked around the room.

"I hear it, but there are no notifications yet," Garret replied.

The others were looking around but couldn't tell where the noise was coming from. There were too many different noises mixed in with it to locate the direction of the vibration. Many sounds seemed to echo around the room; even so, it was easy to discern when something wasn't quite right with the equipment. About that time, Jorge noticed sensors starting to change color on display around where the vibration was coming from. A cluster of yellow triangles briefly appeared before they were replaced with red warning signals.

Jorge called out, "Found it. Looks like a bad cooling fan."

"How bad is it?" Zillah asked.

"I can't tell. It doesn't look like it's in a critical area, but who knows what else is going on," Jorge said.

It could have been fate or just dumb luck. A plastic cooling fan was wedged against a critical circuit board. It bent many of the pins on the board during its rotation. Meanwhile, the fan's tin label made random connections and completed various circuits on the board. Zillah had hesitated just long enough. It wasn't until she was about to call out to the others to shut the system down that something glorious happened.

Zillah's mouth was still half-open, getting ready to verbalize her next instructions when she noticed something was different. Although the sensors had just changed color in Jorge's view, it hadn't affected any equipment in Zillah's view yet.

Suddenly, she noticed a yellow alert flash then disappear on a segment of equipment. It was easy to see why it was missed. A tiny board rapidly changed states on the displays between normal, warning, and faulty. It was also half-hidden behind other modules performing as expected. When she finally noticed the electrical board's failure light, she briefly glanced at the center of the orb. It was as if time were slowed down in that instant, and everything was in slow motion.

She saw a black spot that was surrounded by a faint green and blue light. Everyone paused in amazement and watched the darkness grow. As they all stood astonished at what was going on, they continued to watch as the darkness consumed the equipment's inner parts. Jorge turned to Zillah,

"Is that what I think it is?"

"I believe it is, Jorge; at least I hope it is," Zillah replied.

"Yes, let's hope it's not the beginning of a complete meltdown," Jorge said.

"Why would you even say that?" Garret asked, frozen with amazement.

Despite any concern, the sleeping beast had come to life. The center was no longer translucent but filled with a black abyss; it seemed to absorb the light nearby as a pulse of energy radiated through the room. Zillah wanted to be careful not to send anything or anyone across till they knew for sure it was safe. After all, they had no idea when or where was on the other side of that darkness. At this point, it was at best a calculated guess.

As they all continued to marvel at what was happening, Zillah caught a bright flash just under the observation window. About that time, the abysmal fluid-like sheet snapped back to the center of the portal. A thin white smoke trail began to rise in front of the window in the bay area below.

"Shut it down, shut it down!" Zillah yelled with excitement.

"I told you that you were going to jinx it," Garret commented as he turned off the last of his components supplying power to the portal.

The Quarksandrium was, in fact, a species of a time machine, although it wasn't the traditional type of time machine, since the device never traveled anywhere. Still, it would open and close a portal into an alternate space and time. The theory had been pursued for many years, but no one had ever come close to making it happen.

Some ideas suggest that since time is the fourth dimension, it travels in a straight line. Zillah's research led her to believe that it wasn't straight, but spiraled. If a person were to pick one exact point on Earth and follow it throughout time, it would be a never-ending line that never traced itself. When stepping away from the picture, it is actually similar to an unrolled spool of wire.

Many philosophers had mapped the universe successfully but failed to account for the universe moving among galaxies. Their timeline was like a spiral phone cord, strung symmetrically around a living room in tiny circles, then larger circles. It was often difficult to gauge unless a person had a specific point of origin to calculate other periods.

Zillah had an unusual perception of time. She also had an extra sense of time and space around her, even equating it to mathematics. However, others had trouble comprehending her formulas. She designed a map referencing particular landmarks with unconventional continuum markers. It was a long process she had begun in the first ten years of the Quarksandrium project. Although she deciphered only a postage-stamp-sized area of space travel, it was enough to extrapolate a formula for all time travel. Computers would be able to use the formula to visit anywhere on the timeline based on their current position.

Zillah had orchestrated the construction of the building in which her lab was the centerpiece. The design was made so that every January first, the building's design would shift to a different pattern to distinguish a new year. Although the construction started on a smaller scale, segments were added each year that added many more departments and research areas. Subsequently, the roof was designed with a much different pattern design than the inside of the building.

The building's architecture was intricate, with moving parts like walls, corridors, rooms, and even plumbing. It was would have been inconceivable hundreds of years ago. This building and its design were the first measurable markers of time in Zillah's time architecture.

As the years passed and the project neared the testing phase, Zillah realized that the lines where time overlapped themselves were far more significant than she had initially calculated. Time seemed to compound into a spiral helical shape that simulated Earth's path in orbit around the sun, universe, and galaxy. One could almost view it as the DNA of Earth.

The machine was designed to cross the stitch of time closest to their current time and position. These overlapping time paths were when specific points crossed an earlier trail of time left behind by Earth. They often called the time overlaps "time shadowing." Since time always moved forward, this limited the travel generally less than ten years. Any time beyond the shadow would require significant space travel to reach Earth.

When something crossed into the shadow, communications were severed, other than leaving a historical data trail to view in the future. Safety was one of Zillah's primary concerns for her team and the time continuum itself—not only the safety of the individuals but the safety of the timelines. Although there were a lot of theories, none were proven at this point.

After the excitement of the first signs of life with the portal, Zillah went on an expedition to find where the smoke had come from.

"Well, it looks like we need to redesign this circuit board," Zillah said as she waved around a blackened board from one of the cage panels.

"It looked like someone kicked the exhaust fan housing, and it was smashed against the board. I don't know if I should be mad or thankful. It might have taken us another year or two to figure this issue out."

"That's crazy! The fan must have been what made the sensors freak out and give intermittent garbage data," Jorge said with an aha moment.

"I wonder how the case got bent," Garret commented, feeling as though it were his fault.

Zillah brought the team together to extrapolate the data gathered from the portal opening. They found that one board just couldn't replicate what the fan was doing to the board when the portal opened, so they replaced it with three more advanced circuit panels. After testing the process one more time, they opened the doorway once more for three minutes before closing.

When they were finally ready for their first mission, Zillah commented to the team as they powered on the units, "Let's not have any meltdowns today, please. And no funny accents."

As they neared a similar stage as the first run, the abysmal fluid flowed from the orb in the center until it reached the portal's outer frame. Ravyn continued to follow Zillah's instructions and document what she did. Still, she was also tasked with moving a large robotic arm through the portal with a camera attached.

"OK, I'm going to move the camera through the plane," Ravyn said nervously.

The camera moved through the portal's center's abysmal fluid and disappeared to the other side. The team would use the footage to pinpoint exactly where in time the machine had shadowed.

There were many safety measures in place to prevent engineer contact with the fluid. Several scanners patrolled the outer edge of the portal. Any human tissue would automatically close the gap before contact was made.

She maneuvered it slowly through the frame into the abysmal substance until it gradually swallowed the entire camera. Ravyn continued holding the robot steady even though it felt like there was a strong wind on the other side. The portal was stable less than three minutes before the shadow path would be out of range, and the portal would close.

"Retracting the camera," Ravyn said.

"Alright, people, that's a wrap. Good mission. Let's shut it down," Zillah announced.

There were a few cameras lost in space and the ocean on the next few missions because they lost track of the shadow clock. Since the portal was able to venture only within the recent decade, the severity of losing equipment was minimal. The three scientists and the steady intern continued on their path, gathering critical information to extend the time travels' parameters and abilities.

It wasn't until the eighth mission, several weeks later, that they came across their first large anomaly. With twenty seconds left till the portal would cross the shadow threshold and close, the arm retracted, and the camera emerged from the dark liquid-like substance created from the portal's center.

"Why is the camera wet?" Ravyn asked.

"That's kind of strange. I know it's fluid-like, but it's never left a residue before," Jorge said. Fortunately, they had used weatherproof cameras, but as they connected the camera to the monitors to play the footage, they saw only white. At first, they thought the camera was ruined, and it had recorded only white noise.

"Wait, what is that?" Garret pointed out as they watched the footage.

"I can't tell. It looks like something moving. Maybe it wasn't a busted mission after all," Jorge replied.

"It looks like some sort of lights, or..." Ravyn began guessing what the objects could be.

"I think it's a highway," Zillah said with a hint of doubt.

Occasionally there were faint images of tall structures, silhouettes of transportation bridges, and even communication tower lights flashing in the distance. They hadn't seen a snowstorm like this before.

"How did we travel that far back? There hasn't been significant snow since before the Quenomoly," Zillah asked as the others watched the screen intently.

"It is strange. Do you think there's another short somewhere?" Jorge questioned.

The Quarksandrium had worked, but it was supposed to cross only into recent time shadows within the last decade. Zillah's eyes began to cross as her vision unfocused through the flying snow. *How could this spectacular anomaly happen? Was there another accident that caused it to stray further back in history from the current timelines?* Many questions filled Zillah's mind as to how this result could have come about.

She stayed late into the night, trying to figure out what had happened while the others went home. She thoroughly searched every piece of equipment until there was only the orb to inspect. She opened the center of the great machine to find a pyramid-shaped relic wedged inside, held by a piece of red square cloth. It didn't belong there, and she had never seen it before. After removing the lodged article from the machine and returning it to normal, she concealed it in her pocket and never told anyone else.

The next day, Zillah schedule a meeting with the board that oversaw the Quarksandrium project to describe the situation. She explained that the Quarksandrium was functional, but it could cross only to parallel times. It wasn't often that someone had the prestige to go in front of the board. Although this wasn't her first time seeing them, it was always an intense and unique experience.

They weren't like most people, or even beings, for that matter. Zillah looked with concern and intensity at the board so they would take her seriously as someone who knew her field of study. Like any members of a commission, the board members varied in size and personality. Still, they all appeared in similar robes, suits, and clothing. Three had green suits, almost grass-like in color, which is sort of tacky to the touch, but strangely enough, was never dirty. The green-suited beings sat at the end of the table closest to her, which was near the door.

It was hard to focus sometimes on what she was supposed to be talking about when her mind wandered to such weird things. Three more members were wearing crimson suits with flowing, loose-fitting crimson robes, sitting near the head of the table. All the members' faces were covered with similar exosuit helmets, including the dark eyes that couldn't be seen. In fact, the only member without a mask was the person leading the meeting.

The board was a faction of the government. Many of these beings appeared the century after the Quenomoly. Their skin also appeared to mimic their surroundings at times. It was generally known that they were nearly impenetrable to knives, bullets, and lasers. She wondered if this was how people of the past had thought aliens would look. But were they really aliens or something else? Nobody really knew the answer to that. It could be that their technology was how the exosuits came into existence.

The leader of the board realized that the project would require the assistance of the Parmathians. The Parmathians came to this planet within the last couple of decades from what some believed was a parallel dimension or distant planetary system. It was their technology that was needed to specify which point in time they would need to travel. The lead board member looked at Zillah,

"You must go meet with Goramaius. He has the technology you will need to complete the Quarksandrium."

Zillah turned without saying anything and walked to the door. It was strange that the board didn't seem to need this technology when they showed up, yet they also appeared from nowhere as if they were from another time and dimension. The second in command stood and retrieved a package from the nearby cabinet.

"Zillah!" he called. Zillah turned as she caught a box covered in strange symbols from the corner of her eye.

"A gift for your travels. It will become clear in your journey why you will need these…

"…follow the scorpion," he said.

The next few weeks, Zillah and her husband prepared their gear and baggage for travel. The Parmathians lived under the hills in the Ozarks just south of what used to be Branson, Missouri, centuries ago. The next morning, they packed the vehicle and left Eirwen with friends, watching their house until they returned. She was about ten at the time. Eirwen knew they were going because of work but didn't realize how dangerous the journey would prove.

THE JOURNEY

As they finished loading their vehicle and said goodbye to Eirwen, Zillah took a deep breath and looked off into the distance through one of the garage windows.

"Are you OK?" Jorge asked in a concerned voice.

"Yes, I must just be anxious about finding the missing piece," Zillah said as she tried to reassure herself that everything would be OK.

"I understand. I have faith it will work out how it is supposed to, though," Jorge said, trying to comfort her. But for some reason, Zillah wasn't at ease with the journey. Something didn't feel quite right. As they closed the van's doors, Zillah pressed the button to release the seals on the garage. The door released a gasp as the polluted air rushed in, hugging the van. Since the ban on vehicle transportation inside the city, not many people required vehicles unless they were traveling great distances or had elevated government privileges. Even then, there were other types of transportation.

A green hue engulfed the vehicle's bottom as Jorge pushed the button to engage the van's engine. As it lifted off the ground, dust and contaminated air swirled together, rolling like waves from underneath, until the van reached its height a couple feet above the ground. Jorge moved the throttle, and the vehicle began to inch forward out into the open.

Light began creeping into the van, engulfing its cabin as they continued moving out of the garage. Zillah moved to put her hand on Jorge's leg and looked over at him with a stare that would take the breath away from any man. When Jorge turned his head to look over, Zillah muttered in a soft suggestive voice,

"Maybe we will get some special time together."

Jorge instantly realized what she was talking about as he caught his breath and tried to regain composure, squirming a little in response to an uncomfortable pinch. Zillah's anxiety had obviously changed to something more intimate.

Jorge leaned over and kissed Zillah. "Yes, I think we will have plenty of time for that."

With nothing more, Jorge turned and exited the driveway. Zillah stared out the windshield as the distant sign grew larger as they approached. *Thanks for Visiting Artesia,* which had been their home in New Mexico for many years since they started the Quarksandrium project.

Jorge was content with driving the distance as he watched the heads-up display shown on the windshield. The instruments showed seven hundred and one miles left until they arrived, which was about five and a half-hour trip. As they neared the town's edge, the virtual road lofted into the sky; the GPS had already plotted the best route to Missouri.

Jorge leaned over briefly to adjust the controls as the van ascended higher from the ground. He seemed focused when pressing the navigational buttons, changing the thermostat, and finally engaging the autopilot that would guide them to their destination.

Momentarily, Jorge's hand glided back from the console to Zillah's knee, then gently up her leg. Zillah briefly closed her eyes, then released a short sigh as she put her hand on his and gently moved it back toward her knee. She gave a look with her eyes and tilted her head while patting his hand, then said, "Only a few more hours, and we'll be there. We better look at the plans for the trip."

"Must you do that to me, again?" he replied, letting out a sigh and shaking his head.

She stretched behind the seat and grabbed what looked like a foot-long shiny cylinder that was a computer scroll. Jorge raised an eyebrow, then returned to his normal seated position. She pinched the middle of the tube with a tab emerging and pulled as a flat transparent page appeared from the scroll. Holding the cylinder and the edge of the page, Zillah gave the page a short, brisk shake. The material stiffened, and a menu appeared. As she guided her fingers over the material, guidelines, objectives, and maps appeared as they had been magically conjured from her mind.

Since weeks of planning had gone into this trip, Zillah wanted to make sure they wouldn't make any mistakes. As they flew over the landscape in their final hour of the journey, they watched the horizon filled with the barren empty carcasses of machinery and what used to be well-kept homes, grocery stores, and bustling city life.

"That must be Oklahoma below us. It's such a wasteland. It really makes me sad, realizing the people who live there don't have anywhere else to go," Zillah said.

"You can tell they tried rebuilding it, but I don't know how that mess of construction is livable. Think about all the tornados and the harsh environment they have to deal with," Jorge replied.

"Where do they even get food or supplies in the countryside? Nothing is protected out here," Jorge continued.

Over the decades, many structures evolved into a hodgepodge of makeshift materials and a never-ending cycle of sick and dying people. It wasn't suitable to live in, considering the state of the environment with radiation winds combined with bio-contaminants.

"I really feel for them, but I just don't understand why they stay. It's not suitable or safe to live there. It breaks my heart they wouldn't think about their kids," Zillah said.

Gentle tones and whistles sounded as Jorge began scanning the countryside.

"It looks like we're about there. The car is descending," Jorge remarked.

"At least we didn't have to drive one of those old cars abandoned down there on the freeway. Think about how long that would have taken us," Zillah replied.

There were two issues with landing in uncharted territory. One was the terrain, the other was the lack of road mapping. Most populated cities had been remapped in the years after the event, but cars still littered the freeways like abandoned salvage yards. Many roads and highways were closed for travel after the comet encounter. With about five miles left, they intensely scoured their surroundings for potential threats.

"It should be up on the left, Zillah," Jorge informed her with an unsure voice. "Are you sure these are the correct coordinates?" he asked as they crawled to a stop.

There were no visible entrances, no signs, and no-one to ask for directions. The rolling hills were covered with trees and occasional clearings of exposed rock. Remnants of housing and partial walls were occasionally scattered across the hillside.

It was rare to see a house that was still intact and inhabited. Sporadically broken and shredded highways were lifted in the air. They held abandoned cars and carcasses of human remains of those who tried to escape the toxic air.

As they sealed their suits and exited the vehicle, they gathered their gear and let the scroll guided them. Even though it didn't look like there was anything around. It seemed like they walked for miles over large rocks and rugged terrain. Zillah grabbed a scanner out of her bag to help them find the entrance as they approached a large rock face.

"So, do you think there will be a big welcome party or just kind of like that last highway we passed over?" Jorge asked with a snarky tone.

"Come on, Jorge, they wouldn't have sent us here if he wasn't still alive," Zillah replied.

They continued along the rock face, seeking the entry point that would eventually give them answers to the questions they had.

"It looks like the rock isn't as deep over here. But how do we get in?"

Jorge began looking through their assortment of tools for something that might help them navigate the entrance.

"Zillah, what's that glowing? Isn't that the artifact box you got from the board? Why is it glowing? I don't remember seeing it like that. Did you do something to it?" Jorge rambled with a barrage of questions.

"Yes, it is. I don't know, and no... I didn't. And what's with all the questions? You know as much as I do at this point," Zillah said. She carefully removed the box from her supply bag. The box was about ten inches long, and its width and height were precisely half its length. It was covered in strange hieroglyphs. The peculiar symbols seemed to be glowing but not consistently. Waves of lights cycled in a single motion from one corner of the box to the other. As Zillah put the box in front of her, she noticed the light patterns change slightly.

"Maybe it's interacting with our location or something else nearby?" Zillah asked with confusion. As they walked, the lights emanating from the glyphs seemed to flow from the direction they needed to walk. It was almost like a beacon, summoning them to a specific point along the wall. They continued walking along the rock face as the lights cycled from one side of the box to the other. As they moved closer to the entrance, the light shifted a bit toward the center of the box. After they had been walking for a while, the box was emanating light from the center inscription outward.

"Well, I guess that means we're here," Jorge exclaimed with both eyebrows raised and a slight tilt of the head. They began to search the wall for clues that would let them inside when the box Zillah held suddenly clicked and gave off a gasp. Zillah's eyes widened as the top cracked open.

"Jorge, the box just opened," Zillah said with a rise in her voice. Briefly, there was the familiar swirl as the two different types of air met each other. She opened the lid to see what it contained. Inside there were three items surrounded by cloth-covered foam that secured each relic.

One was a solid staff about four inches long and an inch wide. A cube about four inches square was to the right of the short staff. What looked like an amulet, or maybe a strange coin, rested in the space that remained. It also seemed to be about four inches across. Upon further inspection, she noticed four empty corners extending beneath the coin. As she removed the coin, her eyes widened when she realized the shape beneath it was an upside-down pyramid. She wasn't sure whether to say anything to Jorge or just keep quiet.

"I should have told you before," she began.

"What are you talking about? Did I miss something? Is this about the touching earlier?"

"No... There's an empty space under the coin," Zillah said shaking her head with a grin. She reached in the duffel and retrieved the pyramid she had hidden when they packed for the trip.

"I found this pyramid in the center of the machine, lodged in a tiny space with a piece of cloth. I think it's what altered the time shadow on the last mission," she explained.

"Are you kidding me? Why didn't you tell me?" Jorge's frustration began to climb, and he was noticeably irritated.

"I... guess I was consumed and thought I should keep it quiet. It didn't make sense at the time," she responded.

"Look, we're in this together. You may have started this project before we met, but we're a team, and we need to trust each other completely, or none of this will work," Jorge said with frustration, but he wanted to point out that he was in it for the long haul. "Let me help," he said.

Jorge reached for the pyramid she was holding and caressed her hand as she released her grip. He placed it in the box, and she returned the coin above it. They once again exchanged looks as they embraced each other, signaling that they would both be OK. All the relics inside were covered in different glyphs, similar to those on the outside of the box.

They lost focus on the box during their brief emotional eruption. Yet, after returning the pyramid and coin to the box, the cylinder's markings began to glow. Zillah removed the short wand from the artifact box. She could actually feel the energy it contained, through her suit. The rod appeared to be made of some sort of stone. As she moved the wand horizontally across the horizon, she noticed that the glow got stronger in certain areas. Gravitating toward where the light was most potent, she found herself closer and closer to the wall of rock.

"I have to say, even with all the technology we have, this artifact is pretty cool. I can't get over how the pieces just guide us to the next step. Feels like we're tracing the path of a Freemason," she said with excitement.

As she neared, she noticed that there was a faint glow coming from the wall, as well. After handing the box to Jorge, she brushed her hand across the face of the rock where the light was escaping. As the dust created a cloud and fell to the ground, the same symbol she uncovered appeared on the end of the wand. The rod's end was shaped differently from the rest of the stick, but the odd shape fit precisely with the two matching symbols.

Her hand shook slightly from the adrenaline of the unfamiliar situation. The two characters glowed more intensely as they neared each other, till the magnetic force drew the rod from her hand. And just like that, the rock released the vacuum of air it had sealed behind it, sucking in dust and debris from the outside.

A large swath of rock gave way and moved inside the hill as if it were swallowing it whole. The rock face moved to reveal a large room with several corridors branching off the main room. Zillah retrieved the rod from the rocks, returning it to the cradle inside the box.

"I guess we're supposed to use the cube now, because it's giving us a light show," Zillah said. She pulled the square stone from the box and noticed that only one side was lit. There were three paths to choose from that branched off the main room.

"The cube has to be the map, but how do we decipher it?" Jorge asked.

They flipped and turned the cube to figure out if there was a pattern to the dim glow shining through the cube. Zillah noticed while turning the cube that the underside had a picture of a scorpion scribed on it and was glowing the strongest.

"The board guy said, 'Follow the scorpion.' This must be what he meant," Zillah said.

"Let's just go down one of the tunnels and see what happens," Jorge said hastily. As they walked toward the tunnel on the left, the cube began to grow noticeably dimmer, barely emitting light at all.

"I think we should try a different path," Zillah suggested.

As they crossed the room, Zillah stumbled on a crack, disturbing the earth covering a large design. Suddenly, light pierced through the dirt on the floor.

"...and there it is..." Zillah said with a haughty taunt. They brushed the ground and found a more magnificent scorpion, identical to the cube. Soon, both began flashing lights synchronously.

"That must be the way," Jorge said assumingly.

Leaving the entryway, they began the long walk down into the tunnel. It was a quick descent, and the pair continued deeper down into the depths of the corridor. The clean-cut tunnel gradually became more obstructed with large rocks that got wetter and more slippery the deeper they went. It was much darker here than it was closer to the surface. Algae covered the rocks along their sides and edges.

"Eeaaaahhhgggh!" Jorge yelled, and Zillah immediately stopped.

"What happened? Are you OK?" Zillah asked.

"I think I'm OK. My foot slipped when I was walk-ing across the water stream. I'll be OK. I probably just sprained my ankle," Jorge replied in pain.

"It looks like you did more than that. Your suit is torn, and you're bleeding down your leg. I'll get a ban-dage," Zillah said. She quickly but calmly dug into her bag and grabbed various liquids to clean the wound and bandage Jorge's leg.

"This is probably going to sting a little," she said.

"Aaaargggh, yeah… just a little," Jorge screamed as he tried to breathe through it but still pulled away from the pain. She wrapped the wound with gauze and a liberal amount of tape.

"Just a little more tape to make sure it doesn't get contaminated."

"OK, OK, that's good. Let's keep moving. I'll be fine," Jorge continued, being insistent.

As they climbed over and around the large rocks, they could see the tunnel widened and got brighter again as it opened to another large room. Zillah ap-proached the opening with Jorge limping behind. It looked just like the rest of the structure until they en-tered the grand room and saw the architecture. The expression on both their faces seemed to ask *How is this possible?*

"How did they do this? It's magnificent! Look at all the carvings in the stone. We have to be at least a mile from the entrance," Jorge said, wincing through the pain.

Large columns and intricate carvings covered several walls and pillars. The dirt floor turned into large marble squares. A beautiful water feature trickled down a massive piece of art in the corner of the room. Two large doorways accentuated the columns on the far wall. As the two stood in awe of the majestic space, a booming voice appeared from one of the openings.

"I hope your journey wasn't too treacherous."

Zillah and Jorge froze for a moment just before they saw a shadow moving through one of the doors. Then a large figure moved into the light. He was of average height yet muscular, dressed in what looked like an emperor warrior suit. Blue and red sashes danced and hugged his armor plating. He also wore a mask that contained a respirator with blue-tinted lenses covering his eyes. Although he didn't walk far, it seemed he had an abnormal gait to his walk, perhaps from a warrior injury.

"I have been expecting you," he said as his peculiar voice echoed through the chamber. "Follow me."

Jorge and Zillah cautiously walked toward him as he turned and retreated through the doorway. They continued down a short hallway and noticed a flickering light coming from the room ahead. As they entered the room, a long table sat in front of them with long benches on each side and a larger chair at the table's head. As the ruler sat in the head seat, he spoke with surety.

"You may have guessed, I am Goramaius. I have

been here for some time but was born in Parmathius. Have a seat. A meal has been prepared for you," the ruler said commandingly.

The two hesitantly sat down at the table.

"Do not worry, the air is safe here. Your masks are not required for these quarters. It is pressurized beyond the waterway to circulate fresh air. You may not have noticed, but you walked through a force field that contains the atmosphere in the tunnels," Goramaius reassured them.

Jorge pushed the button sequence on his arm and removed his headgear, then Zillah followed. It wasn't until they released their head apparatus that they heard the faint sound of music playing from other parts of the cavern. Both participants filled their plates and began to eat the feast that was prepared. The conversation was sparse as the two continued to finish their meals.

"I hope you enjoyed the meal. Let us go to the library, and I will gift you that for which you have come," Goramaius offered with generosity. He led the way to an adjacent room with a long wall of books and the opposite wall filled with magnificent artwork. Each painting seemed to glow with light, as if a spotlight were shining on it. However, there was no light source to be found. Near the end of the room was a large wooden desk made of a deep-colored walnut. It was clean, with not one scratch anywhere to be seen. Nothing was cluttering the desk's top, either.

Goramaius walked behind the desk. Squatting

down, he retrieved an object from a drawer and placed it in the middle of the desk. It looked like a multi-sur-faced orb with many flat triangle sides. It spanned about a foot in diameter and had a radiant cyan glow glistening from its triangle edges. Each of its triangles had some sort of hieroglyphic symbol inside it. As Zillah gravitated toward the entrancing object, Goramaius commanded her.

"Stop!"

Immediately she lifted her head from the orb to Goramaius. She could feel the intensity of his facial expressions from behind the mask, even though they weren't visible.

"I thought you said this is why we are here," Zillah replied with confusion.

Goramaius held his hand out, waiting for his bounty.

"The box, kindly surrender the box," Goramaius said as he stretched out his hand.

Zillah removed the bag from her shoulder and put the bag down on one of the nearby reading chairs. Reluctantly, she pulled the box out of the pouch and placed it in his hand.

Carefully, Goramaius walked behind the desk again, resting the chest behind the orb on the desk. He opened the box and raised the medallion, scrutinizing it meticulously as if it were a precious stone. It was the same size as the one around his neck, which looked strangely similar.

Goramaius briefly looked up, then held the amulet

around his neck in one hand and the medallion in the other. As he flipped the amulet to its back, he brought the two together and gave it a small twist. They heard a click and a brief pulse of energy emitted from the objects. As he looked to the ceiling, he released them to dangle from his muscular neck again.

Goramaius took a deep breath, as if the trinkets gave him an extra boost in his lungs. The energy he gained seemed to make him stand a little taller. It was almost like a drug that he craved but had not felt in a long while. When he regained his composure, he pushed the orb on the desk toward Zillah.

"It is yours. Be wise, and use it only for good. Some things you cannot change from the past. Some of the past is based on your future, and parts of both can never be changed," the ruler concluded, sharing his riddle as he turned and looked at the large painting that hung behind the desk. With that, Zillah retrieved the Quarksandrium orb from the desk and carefully placed it in her bag that previously held the chest. Zillah continued securing the large orb in the bag just as Goramaius turned to face the adjacent wall. It was almost as if he were dealing with an internal battle of whether to allow her to accept the relic.

"You won't last out there if your leg isn't treated first. Follow me," Goramaius said.

He turned sharply from the wall and passed them, exiting the room. Jorge and Zillah followed the strange-ly acting leader. They weren't sure why they trusted him, but they had a feeling their best interest was his concern. Walking across the dining area, Jorge commented on the feast they had moments ago.

"Where did it all go?" Jorge asked.

"That's just weird," Zillah replied.

They hadn't heard any footsteps, dishes clanking while being removed, or any other sounds while they were in the library. Yet the table was pristine, without a trace that they had even sat down. Only a running cloth remained down the center of the table, with fresh unlit candles. Bewildered, they continued following the unfazed leader through a large door with tinted glass.

Upon entering the room, they noticed a very clean smell. The unmistakable smell of ozone lingered in the room, and the bright light was a very intense contrast to the dark rooms next to it. The two squinted to shield their eyes until they adjusted to the bright light. A row of white cabinets lined the wall on one side of the room; it was evident that it was a medical room. The countertop was cleared except for one stainless steel tray in the center. It contained only a syringe and a vial of some translucent bluish-green substance.

"I noticed you injured your leg. This will prevent you from contracting anything. Remove your bandage, and we can get it dressed up," Goramaius said insistently.

He opened cabinets and retrieved various cleaning materials and fabrics. Zillah began helping Jorge remove the bandages they applied earlier. Goramaius removed the sheath from the needle and filled the syringe with the green liquid. He turned slowly with his head bowed, then knelt as he injected the fluid beside the wound.

As Jorge winced in pain, Goramaius commented, "This injury will be with you longer than you expect, but you will persist." Goramaius then disposed of the needle and retrieved bandages that made a much better wrap than the previous set. After applying it, it was hard to distinguish where the wrap began, and the suit started.

"I wish you both safe travels to your destination."

Goramaius reached to hold Zillah's hand and moved it to his mask as if he were kissing it, then held out his hand toward the door, ushering them out.

Zillah and Jorge shouldered their bags and began walking toward the door. Since Jorge was still in pain and not feeling the best, he rested a hand on Zillah's low back. It was partially to make her speed up but also to help with his balance. As they left the dining area, they engaged their helmets to provide the life support they required in the unfriendly atmosphere. Retracing their steps, they made their way over the large slippery rocks, even though Jorge struggled with his injured leg. Soon they began their climb up the steep hill to the surface. Jorge's limp got increasingly worse and continued to throb until he frequently took breaks.

"I can't tell if my leg is itching from the shot he gave me, or if I'm just hot from the pain, but something is definitely happening," Jorge exclaimed.

"I'm sure it will be OK. Goramaius seemed genuine, but I did notice him hesitate before he gave you the shot," Zillah said.

They continued on the journey to the car when Jorge asked, "What did he mean by some of your past depends on your future?"

Zillah gave it some thought and shook her head.

"I'm not sure. It didn't make much sense to me either. It was an odd choice of words, though, don't you think?"

Zillah helped Jorge up the remaining incline as he hobbled along. As they exited the hillside, the large stone wall closed behind them. It sealed the hidden lair and prevented their return. They were finally out of the cavernous hillside, but they still had quite a trek to get to the vehicle.

The sun was no longer lighting the way, since many menacing clouds had moved in during their visit with Goramaius. They hoped the rain would hold off till they returned to the van. Just as Zillah was about to comment on the weather, it got noticeably colder as sprinkles began to fall.

"Almost there. Let's get you some help for that leg," Zillah said, expressing concern.

After closing the doors to the van, they breathed for a few minutes in relief at being in a warm place again and watched the rain hit the windshield. It covered the glass in a blurry hue of green, almost like an old Coke bottle.

Raindrops began hitting the window in the hospital room that momentarily brought Zillah back to the present and the conversation she was having with Eirwen. She didn't often let her thoughts flurry in the past in such detail. Still, for some reason, her mind trailed in many directions around the Quarksandrium project, along with the good and bad times she had spent with Jorge.

As Eirwen continued on about other thoughts and stories of her life, Zillah retrieved a deck of cards from a nearby ledge and began to shuffle. They often played gin to occupy their hands while they were talking. Zillah passed out the cards as her memories began to flood back. Project recovery was what gave her a foothold with Zander Enterprises before the Quarksandrium project was created.

PROJECT RECOVERY

As she drifted back into thought, Zillah pondered how it must have been on earth after the Quenomoly. The once blue marble that glowed with life was a beautiful sight from anywhere in space. A tiny shimmer from afar became a gift from God and visual jubilation the closer and larger it got. It was a marvel of a magnificent feat that he had created such a beautiful place for humans to thrive. During their time, people had overcome adversities to create things that were once thought to be impossible.

Each step greater than the last. Some never thought it would be possible to land on the moon, not to mention Mars. Though man failed when they tried to reach God and his glory in the heavens, the tower of Babel fell. Still, mankind reached new heights when they were humbled before the Lord. The difference wasn't to gain godly power but to explore, understand, marvel, and live in all that God created while worshiping him through his son Jesus.

Earth was not just a small marble in the middle of

the vast dark ocean of space. It was the center of life. After all, why create galaxies if humans were to never see or reach them? The Quenomoly had brought unspeakable change to Earth. No longer was the vibrant blue sphere visible the way it once was. In the months following, a dark emerald haze swirled around the entombed planet, stifling its glow. The sun was shunned and filtered by a green lens nobody had seen before. Although it wasn't as dark or dense as the initial overlay, it never returned to how it had been created.

Back in the third decade of the year two thousand, Gretta was more fortunate than her coworker Jim had been after the comet strike. The same leaders that had abandoned Jim seemed to think Gretta would provide a valuable set of skills. Perhaps they chose her because of her more rigid posture, neat appearance, or smooth-talking demeanor when she spoke to people. Sometimes the appeal of a person's beauty went farther than knowledge, resourcefulness, or even persistence.

She was studying the events on Mars in the years after when she made a discovery.

"Mr. Clumbly, Mr. Clumbly, look at this! I found it. It's amazing. I noticed this from a Mars rover that was still intact after the comet strike," Gretta said with enthusiasm to the new czar of space exploration.

"What did you find, Gretta?" the director questioned.

"Since Mars has changed orbit, I've noticed a lot of change in the terrain. The rover sensors indicate that the temperature has risen and several other anomalies that I can't explain," Gretta said.

"What anomalies would those be exactly?" the czar continued questioning.

"Oxygen levels have spiked, and it appears there is a stable atmosphere. I don't see any plant life yet, but if there's oxygen, there has to be water, too. I can only imagine the change will continue, and it will be suitable for habitation soon," she said with excitement.

"As you know, designs for balloon pods and transport ships have been underway for deep-space transport. If this is true, it might not be such a long journey after all," Clumbly replied.

"I will keep you updated, sir," Gretta said.

Initially, Mars would still be just as uninhabitable as earth. But over the next several years, the large red planet would undergo changes that would open a whole world of opportunities—literally.

The once red planet started to change in the weeks it got closer to the sun. Over the next few years, the air would stabilize and be as breathable as Earth had been before the Quenomoly. Gretta's discovery from the Mars rover led them to more closely examine the possibility of human migration.

Even though the planet would encounter violent storms in the early years, they would dissipate and calm over time. The red clay and dirt of Mars took on a whole new color as water and storm systems began to form around Mars. It was no longer known as the "red planet." In fact, it was closer to a lively pink. Deep vibrant lakes were coated with bright pink algae, plants began to sprout, water was flowing; it was coming alive. In the years that followed, the president was in close contact with her primary czar, who had a more relaxed tone than before.

"Madam President, Mars is looking more and more enticing, and Space Force is distributing the plans for the balloon pods. The pods should be able to easily navigate a significant portion of the population to the upper atmosphere of Earth into low orbit," the director advised.

"What about the second phase of transporting our colonies to Mars?" she asked.

"We've ascertained a plan that will allow all vaccinated and marked personnel to join the transport ships in low orbit and continue to Mars. It is a phased rendezvous with multiple trips for the transport ships. It should allow Space Force to enforce our laws through space and the new planet," Clumbly explained.

With Mars' new position, it would only take a couple weeks for the transport ships to get to the new planet. Even though Mars wasn't quite like it used to be, humans took delight in the unique opportunity to expand their horizons. Scientists believed that the comet must have contained the right combination of materials to create its own atmosphere around the planet. It was an absolute miracle. The vegetation was nothing like humans had ever seen and followed very few of the same plant patterns. In the years after the incident, exploration teams were sent to document and ascertain whether the new developments were suitable for human life. Eventually, they discovered that it was safe, which led to mass migration to the new planet. It was a chance at a new beginning. To live in the fresh air, under a clear sky, and be free again.

Many people died in the early days before living patterns were normalized. Nobody knew how unlivable the air had become. Protective suits became normal. It looked as though they were preparing to go scuba diving in the early years, except nobody went underwater.

In the years after the comet strike, Space Force distributed plans for low-orbit spacecrafts called balloon pods. People all over Earth worked tirelessly to build balloon-like crafts that would carry hundreds of people just beyond the Earth's atmosphere. The ships were quick and easy to assemble.

"We're ready to launch Project New Hope, Madam President," Mr. Clumbly said.

"OK, this is a massive coordinated effort. The rest of the federation has agreed to launch with our instruction on my command," the president said.

"The transport ships will need to launch first, from the larger cities. Once they are in orbit, we can allow staged docking with the balloons to occur before embarking for the new world," Clumbly said with a sheepish grin.

"This has been a decade in the works. We need to ensure this plan is successful. We must also retain power during the shift between planets. I didn't come this far to hand it over to someone else," the president remarked.

The larger transport ships were constructed in larger cities overseen by leaders of the Space Force division. Although the balloons were more straightforward than the transport vessels, they provided a way for the more common people to meet with the transport ships and the elite that had already abandoned the blue planet.

It was a global effort. Construction plans about building safe ships that would take them to the edge of space began to circulate through camps and cities everywhere. Although they were easy to build, some weren't without fault and didn't make it to their destination. They would transport hundreds of people and many animals in one launch.

The balloons were shaped like flat footballs that were painted silver to reflect the sun's heat. Each balloon was about the size of a football field. In fact, that is where most cities built their balloons. There were two kinds of balloons: oblong ones and round ones. The oblong ones were made on football and track fields, and the round ones were built on softball fields.

The transport ships were much more extensive and built only in significant countries of the world. Each transport ship's size was genuinely massive and could haul several hundred balloons' capacities to the new world. Of the thousands of balloons, there were hundreds of transport ships. It took weeks for the balloons to dock and unload their cargo.

Once the transports were loaded, the final journey began. It was about a month before they would arrive at their destination. Even though the distance was far shorter, the large ships moved considerably slower than smaller crafts.

A beautiful array of sparkling silver dots began to poke through the dense, dark-green atmosphere surrounding Earth. The view from space was quite impressive as the sun reflected off the thousands and thousands of objects that began to shine through the clouds. It was a mass exodus from a planet that had been burnt from a species only trying to survive. Soon after, large transport ships descended to dock with the waves of balloons, waiting for their chance to venture to a new world.

One by one, the balloons docked with the transporters, and families reunited again for the journey to the new land. However, not everyone would exit the hostile environment. Teams of research analysts and other scientific groups stayed behind to create new inventions and continue life on Earth. They rebuilt many cities and started a new way of life in a hostile environment. It wasn't without discord, though. The president made every effort to maintain control of every ounce of power she had gained over the years.

Once the orbital exchange was complete, the balloons were left in Earth's low orbit. Thousands of shiny balloons lingered and danced around Earth like a pond's shimmering water, dancing in the sunset on a beautiful fall evening. Like an abandoned junkyard, they remained until someone came to take them away.

Meanwhile, the remnants of what was left behind on Earth were extreme on both sides of the fence. Many people refused to leave Earth, either because of their religious beliefs, financial status, or duties to the government. Conspiracies became widespread regarding limited supplies, food, and water. Many people believed the government's exit plan was to kill everyone to preserve resources, and Mars wasn't really inhabitable. They lived in caves, makeshift houses, or other shelters they found around the globe.

The next few centuries would prove to be very insightful in how propulsion and transportation would be transformed, from land and personal vehicle travel to mass transit and space travel. New inventions, including compounds, fabrics, and medicine was discovered to combat the changing environment. The Quenomoly had created a whole new platform and a clean slate for inventions.

Zillah's mind eventually brought her back to how it all started with her career at Zander. Project Recovery had been underway for several decades. Still, the process was slow because many of the scientists left behind were studying other things. It didn't seem like a considerable concern, just something that needed to be done eventually.

Zillah was first recruited by Zander Enterprises when she was working as a student. She began as an intern, just like most of Zander's recruits. In its early years, Zander wasn't a well-known company. It wasn't until the coordination of the balloons and transport ships after the Quenomoly that they became widely recognized. Before that, the company had worked silently behind the scenes or with other large corporations, most notably NASA, pharmaceutical, and oil companies, but those changed significantly after the incident.

After graduating, Zillah caught a break and was hired onto Project Recovery as a project manager. They had recovered hundreds of balloons, but there were still thousands more to bring down. She loved working with space projects, so she considered it an excellent opportunity to gain experience and move up the ranks. Each balloon was large, the technology was old, and the manual labor was extensive to recover each balloon.

Project New Hope happened so fast that there was no plan to rescue the ships after they were launched. Project Recovery was the project name of various missions to bring all the ships back to Earth. Clearing launch paths was essential to re-establish shipping lanes to Mars. It was necessary to clean up Earth's orbital debris field so future flights could occur without worrying about collisions.

The early years of recovering balloons required individual ship launches. Each balloon was considered a mission. As the years went by, other efforts were tested to get better and faster results. Ultimately, it came back with the previous results. It wasn't till Zillah acquired the project lead that they finally began to see better results. She designed packs that would retrofit with the balloon's systems. Most of the ships were empty or had very little fuel left. The new system was easily attached and provided them a way to land quickly. Since the new drive systems had advanced in the last fifty years, it made more sense to use up-to-date technology rather than techniques used centuries ago.

Remarkably, she surpassed everyone that had been on this project before her. She had joined the project team only five years ago and already accomplished more than the previous seventy-five years.

Zillah's success with the recovering balloons hadn't gone unnoticed. At the same time, her attention to other, more personal projects also didn't go unobserved. She often burnt both ends of the candle, so to speak. She worked very long days on project recovery, but that never prevented her from spending her nights and often weekends on her own agenda.

When people went home, she would switch to studying time travel and how a machine could open gateways to previous times. She had an extraordinary mind, although she always thought of herself as ordinary and plain. She had the type of beauty that was hidden from most people behind brilliant thinking. Sometimes it came across as insensitive or brutish, but in fact, it was just factual. In some ways, it was what had kept her focused and away from deep relationships, at least until she met Jorge.

A large pop from the heater beneath the window in Jorge's room quickly brought her back to the present. The seasonal rain had stopped and left only a few droplets streaming down the window. As Zillah became aware of her surroundings again and the lackluster conversation with her daughter, the familiar noises of Jorge's equipment flooded in through her ears. She decided to take a walk down the hall and get some water.

"Do you want anything from the machines, Eirwen?" Zillah asked.

"How about a bottle of water and some chips, if you don't mind."

"OK, I'll be right back."

Zillah began walking down the hall to the vending area. Two nurses casually chatted as they briefly stopped to watch her walk past their station. It might have been her paranoia about everything that had happened in her past, but she couldn't shake the feeling that they knew more about the situation than she did.

She paused after retrieving the refreshments from the machines to read the bulletin board that was nearby. *Potluck lunch for nurses in the blue section.* It was slightly overlapping the post below it that seemed like it was more important. *Toy drive for children in long-term treatment.* Most seemed like everyday events with people trying to stay upbeat. Of course, there were occasional items for sale or people searching for various types of services. It was a hodgepodge of listings people around the hospital tacked to the board to inform others of what they were doing. Zillah gathered the chips and water and began making her way back to the drab room Jorge stayed in.

"Here, Eirwen, your chips and water," Zillah said, handing her the items.

"Thanks," Eirwen said nonchalantly.

The two concluded their last hand of cards while they sat with Jorge. The game lasted longer than they had anticipated. Their conversation took many turns that night, including work, Eirwen's upcoming wedding, and what they would do about Jorge being in the hospital. Neither one of them really cared for talking about Jorge's lousy situation, Zillah especially. It brought back too many memories of what her father had been through when she was young. She desperately wished that her daughter hadn't had to go through the same thing she had at such a young age. She knew precisely what Eirwen was going through, but at least she had her fiancé to help her through it.

"What are we going to do without Dad?"

"I really don't want to think about that. I have too

much going on right now," Zillah replied, avoiding the question while placing the deck of cards back where she had found it. Although she avoided the question, she knew it was on the horizon. It was part of the reason she spent so much time at the hospital with him. The amount of finite time she would have with him was better than no time at all. She wanted to absorb every minute. After all, it was his soul that she loved, more than his body.

By now, Jorge was asleep, grunting from pain and gasping for breath. Since he never got quality sleep, he ended up sleeping a lot. The medication kept him in a state that was not coherent to the outside world. Pumps and hoses surrounded him, breathing life into him as long as possible. Spending many nights, for months, Zillah learned to ignore the obnoxious noises of the machines and disgusting sounds from Jorge that would send the casual observer wincing and heading for the door. Eirwen was accustomed to many of these noises, too, as one gets when exposed repeatedly to such monotonous things.

Eirwen could tell her mom was tired and needed some time with her dad. Besides realizing that they had talked about everything that was on her mind, Eirwen didn't know what else to talk about. She packed up what few belongings she had, to make a quiet exit, but pausing before leaving, Eirwen crossed in front of the bed and went to her mom, giving her a long embrace.

"I love you, Mom. Thanks for spending time with

Dad and me tonight. I always enjoy the time we get, even if it's not in the best places."

"I love you too," Zillah said with a heartfelt goodbye.

It was all that Zillah could get to come out. Of the multitude of other thoughts, worries, and apprehensions, that was all she could muster. As Eirwen left the room, she sat back down beside her husband. She intended to stay for only a few extra minutes, but once she grabbed his hand, the comfort settled in, and she began to nod off. Zillah began to enter into another sleep with heavy thoughts about the journey that brought them there. Much like an unfinished novel, it would haunt her until she completed the book.

THE QUARKSANDRIUM DESIGN

She drifted further into a slumber as her mind reflected on how the project evolved over the years. Zillah never seemed to let go of its development, especially since Jorge's health started declining. Her fascination with time travel grew over the years. The promise for fixing significant issues in the past was still evident. Yet, gaining knowledge from historic minds was at the forefront of her mind. For her, it was almost like a distant goal instead of a monumental achievement.

Through college, Zillah seemed to absorb information about time travel and various types of physics. She dove into every possible article or conspiracy theory she could find. Whether it worked or not, she was interested in how all the different ideas could be brought together to form a working portal. It was in these obscure thoughts that she found how to create a functional theory, although many of the ideas she found were beyond the realm of possibility.

In the exploration process, Zillah found it wasn't a complete theory she was interested in, but many small pieces of those hypotheses patched together that made the most sense. Many of the ideas she gathered came from Zander computers that housed many centuries of data archives. Although Zillah was fortunate to have the internship with Zander, she had turned that opportunity into a project manager position and time well spent researching and fine-tuning her machine plans.

"Hi, Ms. Cruz, I see you are working late again," a smooth voice called to her.

Mr. Lucas Collins was the lead on the janitorial crew in the building where Zillah was working.

"Hello, Mr. Collins. Yes, I just can't help myself sometimes. I try to shove as much information in my head as I possibly can," Zillah said with a smile.

"Well, I hope you find the information you're looking for. Be careful with how much time you spend here," he whispered to her.

"They like to watch the cameras. I've got in trouble before for lingering around. Have a great evening," Mr. Collins said as he pushed his mop bucket to the next room.

"Thank you for thinking of me. I'll be OK," Zillah replied confidently.

"I know you will. You have a great future ahead of you," Mr. Collins agreed.

She listened to him with a polite facial expression

but put little stock in what he said. Zillah spent countless hours overnight and weekends filling in the gaps that were missing in her schematics. A large piece of the puzzle she found right within Zander. It was kind of strange that she had access to such sensitive information so early in her career.

Sometimes it even seemed as though someone was handing her the pieces she needed to visualize the machine. Every time she reached an insurmountable obstacle in the process, new information would appear. Then she would make extreme leaps in pulling the ideas together. She worked many years in her spare time researching, assimilating processes, fitting all the virtual pieces together to build the portal. Although the name hadn't been established yet, she knew it would be a spectacular machine.

Her work on Project Recovery during the day seemed to overshadow the work on her side project. But the passion she kept inside for her dream allowed her to work long evenings and weekends, maintaining a steady pace and continued progress. Even though there wasn't a name for the project or even a physical machine yet, she wanted to make the time machine work to prevent the Quenomoly. Before long, theories and ideas began to translate into schematics and drawing plans.

One day, Zillah came in early to find a formally typed letter in a plain white envelope on her desk. It had her name at the top and signed "The Board" at the bottom. Immediately before reading the letter's body, her heart jumped to her throat, then back down to her stomach.

"Deep breath," she whispered to herself.

It can't be that bad. She thought. Until she actually began to read the letter. *Please pack all your belongings into the boxes provided. Proceed immediately to the board room and wait for further instructions.* The pit in her stomach just sank to a new level as her heart began to race. She was almost frozen in her path and knew this wasn't good. Frustrated, she packed the few articles she had on her desk and carried the box with her down the hall. She didn't even have time to say goodbye to any of the people she worked with.

Countless thoughts went through her mind. *Was it something I did? Does someone have a vendetta against me? How will I finish this project if I don't even have a job?* It was never-ending. The small squares on the hall floor seemed to blur together after walking down the corridor for what seemed like forever. Her brain numbingly pondered every angle of what was about to happen.

She was so in tune with concern about what was going to happen, she passed the turn to get to the board room a few hundred feet back. She momentarily realized what she had done and just stopped and gazed down the empty hallway. She noticed that a camera in the corner of the hallway monitored the traffic in each direction. Zillah couldn't help but think,

Maybe they were watching the cameras closer than I thought.

It was nearly seven-fifteen in the morning. Most people didn't arrive until eight-thirty. *How could everything be going so well, and all of a sudden come crashing down around me?* She continued her somber walk down the hall, making her way to the board room. Just about when she was making terms with what was inevitably about to happen, she realized she had arrived at the board room.

"Good morning, Zillah. I'm Emersyn from human resources. Just wait here for a moment, and the board will be with you momentarily."

Zillah stood patiently, holding the box she had previously packed, although it was hard to stand still, knowing what was about to happen. The door beyond the conference room was about thirty feet farther down the hall. After a few minutes, she noticed the door open for Mr. Collins, who exited and went in the opposite direction. *I wonder what he was doing.* As the thoughts began to pile on themselves, the door in front of her opened to the conference room.

"You may enter. I will wait for you here," Emersyn said.

Seven people sat around the long rectangular table. Three were on each side, with the leader at the head of the table. Three were female, two were males, and the other two wore suits from head to toe, similar to the exosuits. They were wrapped in burgundy robes with large wavy sashes. At various points, the robe seemed to glow from underneath. They also seemed to move slower and more precisely. Both masked members appeared older, with a slightly different posture, and very different from the others.

"Close the doors, please," a voice said, emanating from the side of the table. Zillah closed the door reluctantly with a grimace on her face due to what she thought was about to happen.

"I am sure you have a lot of questions about the proceedings of this meeting," the lead member began.

"I have no doubt that you know who I am," the leader said, waiting a moment to see if Zillah would respond.

"I'm the Executive Director of Zander Enterprises, Esther Hallaway. We have followed you and your developments for some time. You have done a remarkable job on Project Recovery. When you have used your time to complete it, that is. However, it has come to my attention, and been well documented, that you are not devoting your full time to this project. Therefore, we cannot allow you to continue dividing your attention between this project your personal ventures."

Zillah's eyes began to burn as she resisted showing emotion to anyone. She blinked a few times rapidly to clear the tears from forming. It was getting more difficult to subdue her panic as her heart had jumped back to her throat and getting harder to breathe. Ms. Hallaway continued as Zillah struggled to maintain her posture.

"Zander cannot have you using company resources for personal projects. These are not planned within the roadmap and are a direct violation of our code of ethics. You are officially terminated from Project Recovery. Your replacement has already been advised."

Zillah couldn't hold back any longer as her eyes welled with tears and began streaming down her face. Even after giving the company everything she had, they removed her like any other cog in the machine. The news was not only deflating, but it was humiliating and frustrating. Zillah had no idea where she would go from here. Her passion had got in the way of her duties, but there was no way to change it now. Moving forward was the only option. Zillah began to turn and walk out when she was interrupted by Esther.

"We aren't finished here. I'm surprised you give up so easily," the director said.

Zillah was confused, but she paused and turned back to the board members.

"Although you have violated the terms of your employment agreement, we want to show you leniency. The two new board members are representatives of Ukaron. They joined Zander to expand into a new sector. The project is to be named Quarksandrium," Ms. Hallaway continued, explaining precisely what was about to happen.

"You have been chosen to lead this project since you already have the desire and ability to keep it moving in the direction needed. You will immediately be moved to a new office in the east wing. Once progress reaches the pinnacle and expansions are required, we will direct you on how to proceed. The representative from human resources is waiting in the hall to direct you to your new office. You may consider this your second chance," Ms. Hallaway said sharply.

Zillah couldn't believe what just happened—what a roller coaster of emotions. She went from being fired and no job to her dream job in less than five minutes. It was the best news. Still, she pondered over the two board members that were different from the others. They seemed familiar, yet very different. It was hard to articulate the connection. She was still carrying her box from her old office as she followed Emersyn down the long hallways.

They walked down several long hallways to the opposite side of the building. When they finally neared her new office, Emersyn pointed to the last door on the left.

"Here's your new home, at least for the time being," Emersyn said with a raised eyebrow.

As Zillah quietly walked through the door, she couldn't help but think how much it reminded her of a broom closet. Resting her box of personal items on the desk, she squeezed by the desk to sit in her new chair.

"Do you have any questions for me?" Emersyn asked with a sense of formality.

"Nothing I can think of, thank you," Zillah replied.

"Great. I have some additional paperwork for you to complete for this new position. I will send it over for you to review and sign. Good luck with your new position," Emersyn said as she turned and walked back to her department.

As Zillah sat facing the door adjusting her new chair, she paused a moment when she found a comfortable spot. Something moving caught her eye outside the window. A large excavating tractor was tilling up the land, making room for a new building. The billboard to the side read, *Future home of Zander Building #7.* Her thoughts immediately traced back to memories of her father and his construction job.

"I'm going to make it right for you, Dad," she muttered to herself as she reached out and traced the tractor on the glass with her fingers.

Zillah continued her research right away with a renewed energy. She spent the next several weeks entering and transferring all the notes she had compiled into the digital space Zander gave her in a new computer system.

It took a while to organize all the information from the drives she had kept separate from the network. Each morning began very methodically with her reading the Bible, meditating on the words, and praying, followed by hours of compiling data to create the Quarksandrium.

She wasn't sure who had access to the data she had gathered, but some days she swore that there was extra information that had appeared from nowhere in her folders. It was strange that it was categorized the same way she would have organized it. Zillah often wondered if it was just the artificial intelligence that had helped her out. Zander was known for running AI in the background to facilitate user movements and optimize workloads.

The fantastic thing about Zander Enterprise's artificial intelligence was that it recognized various patterns. It learned how Zillah would input information and solve problems. Eventually, it would verify and suggest conversion algorithms before they were written. It also highlighted mistakes and made suggestions in real time.

While Zillah understood the process of programming and bringing the system together, it wasn't necessarily that she programmed the whole thing. While she worked on the main points that facilitated the program's backbone, the AI would fill in the gaps and complete the logic, although sometimes, it was necessary to tweak some of the logic that the AI had formulated.

Little by little, the drawings of the components and pieces she had gathered began taking form in her virtual construct. In the early years, she would draw a sense of power and strength from the lot outside her window as she watched workers complete each section of excavation of the coming building.

She had also designed a futuristic building to

house the Quarksandrium. She knew the building was a critical piece in bringing the Quarksandrium to life. So, she developed the building's floor plans to coincide with the intricate flow of the portal. As she designed each phase of the construction to accomplish what the portal needed, the crews outside her window appeared to be working on similar projects. At times, she wasn't sure if she was inspiring the workers or the workers were inspiring her. It was an awkward dance they performed, and sometimes she felt like a plagiarist. It never entered her mind how slowly the building was being built.

Weeks turned into months, then years, until Zillah was finally able to monetize the machine she was working on. There were still missing pieces of the portal, but the overall concept of it was nearly complete. Zillah reached a point where the schematics of the machine mattered more than the code.

Much like any project, the early models lacked a lot of function. Yet still, they fulfilled the main objective. Her first goal was to create the device that would open a portal into another time. Some people may have considered this a wormhole. Of course, it would eventually be tested, but these were just the drawings and her vision of what it could become. All of her research from different sources was compiled and translated into a powerful machine with complex code.

She began constructing pieces here and there that would work together with the code she created. It wasn't in any particular order. A random circuit board here to regulate power resources. A small computer there to monitor various sensors. She solved a detail at a time until she had all the pieces to construct the massive puzzle. Even with her expert knowledge of time, there were still anomalies that hadn't been considered.

It had taken her nearly ten years to construct a portal in the virtual world. Even the drawings were theoretical, and nobody knew if it would actually work. Besides, pulling together so many years of knowledge and theories from different scientists, theorists, and people who didn't really know how time worked. Studies had been done, but nobody even considered getting this close. This would be a monumental event, but how did she know it wouldn't be catastrophic? Perhaps it was her faith and understanding in God that would only allow specific things to happen, no matter what she did at any time. Basic truths still remained.

Zillah began contemplating whether it was actually worth the hardship if she couldn't change the Quenomoly. Of all the things she could have done with her life, she chose this life. She sat paralyzed for a few moments while the thoughts infiltrated her, and the weight of the situation took over. The memories of her past fueled her passion for her future. At other times, they haunted her, immobilizing her for hours, deep with thought and reflection.

THE BUILD

Several years after Zillah had been working on the design of Quarksandrium, it was time to erect the building where it would be housed. She worked with an architect to get elements that she wanted throughout the building. Although she had help with some design elements, she wasn't aware that it was already being built, right outside her window.

It was a unique building, to say the least. However, this new building design would take change annually on the inside after being built. Zillah's influence on the structural design made it an ever-expanding building that resembled a rat maze. The design and length of the halls were essential to accommodate the resonance that the Quarksandrium generated.

As she watched out her window, Zillah often wondered if the building she watched every day would look anything like the one she was designing. It wouldn't be till much later that she realized it was her building, and it was being constructed as she dreamt it. For some reason, the board seemed to expedite things like this to keep her on their timeline. She couldn't shake the feeling that things happened more quickly because knowledge from the future enabled it to happen that way.

She had visualized it from the center out, stretching like octopus tentacles down the long winding hallways. Pipes and electricity were routed through the walls in a way so they could move freely annually. The ability of the hallways to change each year was part of its intrinsic design. It was necessary to maintain the portal's harmonic rhythm, offsetting the annual shifts in the cosmos. Some rooms moved, some didn't, but the route taken through the complex would be ever-changing. Even seasoned personnel would find it challenging to navigate without an updated map.

The center of the structure was where the heart of the project would be housed. Zillah's office, three of her coworkers' offices, and eventually the Quarksandrium itself would be in this area. A large bay area was created with the growth potential of the portal in mind. The machine used massive tentacles to distribute its load throughout the halls, stretching to all edges of the building.

Most of these halls were connected with large bundles of unique fiber optics to transport information needed for the portal's operation. Even though standard fiber traveled at the speed of light, Zillah had modified it through her research to travel faster than light, essentially creating an FTL device. The fiber optics used the same technology that arrived with the Quenomoly. Charged particles were filtered from the air and infused in the massive cable bundles. This new type of fiber allowed light to be accelerated through each strand.

The heart of the device, where the actual portal appeared, required a large control room and massive amounts of power. Zillah's office was adjacent to the control room and would have secure access to all the systems.

The portal's bay area was the only thing that remained stationary and never moved. The changing design had many benefits to the project. It provided the correct resonance, but it also provided an additional layer of extra security. The larger the building was, the harder it would be to navigate without a map.

When viewing the structure from above, the building gave the illusion of rotating crops. In fact, the roof was a marriage of different plants that hid the design of its underlying labyrinth of walls. The roof was a bit more challenging to plan. It had large glass panes covering the maze of crops. The top was independent of the level below it but also moved and rotated annually. It gave the illusion that it was directly connected to the walls beneath.

The rows of crops above the building were not all that different from traditional crops in a greenhouse or hydroponic farms. They included corn, beans, and various vegetables. When an aerial picture of the facility was taken, it could be referenced to a specific year in history. The original design was small, but over time, the building grew to nearly a mile wide.

Part of the design of the building was needed to travel in time. Different patterns in the structure would resonate different frequencies down the hallways when the machine was powered on. These frequencies caused an imbalance in the time opening that allowed time to tear between the two parallels. The FTL resonance device's design allowed the machine to offset planetary distribution to create a hole between two periods.

Soon after the construction of the building's first stage, Zillah called together her new team. Hiring for this project wasn't like historical times when people would apply for jobs and be selected on their abilities. It was up to the companies that put them there. It was a company dictatorship that decided where people would go and how they would be compensated. Many things had changed over the last few centuries. Sometimes, this left people feeling unfulfilled, but the slow erosion of corporate freedoms evolved into this forced work practice.

It was a widespread practice to hire people for their academic abilities rather than raw talent and vision. It has long been dismissed of intuition and "common sense." Either a person had skills and moved up, or they didn't and lingered miserably until they figured out how to manipulate the system. Sometimes, this line of thinking led to haphazard sloppiness and mistakes that couldn't be afforded in Zillah's line of work.

She was fortunate to pick her crew from a list of résumés in different departments at Zander. She stuck with established workers that had proven their abilities through previous projects. Garret Blevins was her first pick. He was a mechanical engineer with one other project he had worked on but done very innovative things. She thought Garret would be best to translate her virtual expectations to physical actuality. Shortly after one of the crew finished painting the room, he walked through the door to greet Zillah.

"Hello, you must be Dr. Cruz. I'm Garret, one of your new associates," Garret said as he stretched out his hand in greeting.

"Yes, nice to meet you, Garret," she said, returning the greeting as she shook his hand. They began chatting about the building and how it was designed, when Jorge walked through the door.

"Hi Jorge, how have you been? Nice to see you again. This is Zillah," Garret said, introducing the two.

"Hello Zillah, VERY nice to meet you," Jorge said, greeting Zillah with a smile he was trying to hold back. Even his eyes seemed to greet her with a friendly hello. Zillah paused for a minute with a reserved and cautious look on her brow,

"Hi, Uh... OK. Now that we're all here, we can get started with bringing this project together," Zillah said, averting the awkward greeting.

QUARKSANDRIUM: THE BEGINNING

They all began setting up their computers in Zillah's office. It was set to be an open floor plan that they all could collaborate with discussion when the occasion arose. Zillah was along the far-left wall. The men were slightly farther away on the wall facing the door and the room's right side. Jorge and Garret had worked briefly together on a job when they were going through their internship many years ago. It was a little easier for them to communicate in the first few weeks on the Quarksandrium project. Needless to say, there was some awkward tension between Zillah and Jorge.

What began as typical conversation quickly migrated to banter and sometimes awkward flirting. Jorge had a way of knowing what to say to get Zillah riled up and aggravated or tense, but he also managed to avoid crossing any lines that would push her to straight anger. It was a strange dance between love and anger, but that made it all the more passionate when the time finally came. They went round and round for months before it finally happened…

"Well, good morning. You look even better than I thought you would," Jorge greeted Zillah as he reached over and moved her hair to look into her eyes. As she opened her eyes, she realized it was more than just a fleeting feeling of passion.

"Hi. I think. Was that supposed to be a compliment?" she asked with a groggy voice.

"I'm really glad you're here. I think you'd be beautiful in any light."

"I think maybe you should have stopped with 'good morning,'" she said with a grin.

They embraced again, absorbing the moment of such strange coincidences and passion. They seemed to realize that times like this don't happen often, and they should be treasured. Even the offbeat insulting compliments didn't seem to sting as badly.

The morning turned into afternoon, and they didn't give a second thought to sharing their weekend with each other. Although Zillah and Jorge's instincts and rationalities tried to send them different ways, something stuck between the two. The long weekend of bonding was what ignited a brief lifetime of love. They shared many of their experiences about how they grew up and how they rationalized life. There wasn't too much they disagreed on, considering the rough banter they encountered when they first met. As with any relationship, the negative aspects were brushed over and didn't really seem to matter anymore. It appeared to be more about how they connected rather than what could drive them apart.

The weekend passed in a whirlwind of a blur. The dawn of Monday rolled in briskly as they got ready and made the short journey to building seven.

"Morning. You're here early this morning," Zillah said as she walked through the door.

"Good morning. Yep, I wanted to get this batch of sensors installed in the telemetry systems," Garret greeted Zillah as she entered the room. He hadn't noticed Jorge walking a few steps behind her. About that time, Jorge stepped into Garret's view and sent salutations his way.

"Hey, Garret," Jorge said with an eyebrow raised, like the cat that ate the canary.

Garret looked at Jorge with a strange, puzzled look but didn't comment on the thoughts that were running through his head. He noticed Zillah and Jorge acting a little more complacent in working through issues than on a typical day. There was a sense something had changed, even if Garret never mentioned it to either of them.

The team's work continued on the project as planned, even with many delays and hurdles. It took three months to finish the main components of the portal. The building continued growing outward as the maze became more extensive and more complicated. It required nearly three times as much cable and hoses to accommodate the wall movement they anticipated throughout the building.

It was entering the fall months when Zillah and Jorge decided to get married, after Jorge popped the question. Zillah was already beginning to show a tiny bit of growth from the bundle they would expect in the next six months. Garret agreed to accompany them to witness their vows. Although it wasn't a big production, they did celebrate afterward with a nice dinner.

"I am still impressed you thought to put fresh water and saltwater areas in the building's design. These shrimp are fantastic," Jorge said as they began eating.

"Thank you. I thought it would be a nice perk to have fresh ingredients," she replied.

Zillah often thought of the tiniest details in everything she did. It was partially why she was so successful.

"Well, this past year has been more than I ever expected when I started working for Zander," Jorge said as they finished their meal.

With the coming spring, Zillah birthed Eirwen and greeted her with love. Typically, Zander employees didn't date or get married within the same division, but this was different for some unknown reason. It was almost as if it were expected or preordained. There seemed to be many weird things that Zillah and Jorge noticed but never inquired about while they were employed with Zander. At times it seemed like they were in a bubble, or some kind of experiment, isolated from the world, and everything was taken care of as it happened—almost like magic, or like someone knew it was going to happen. It was more than eerie at times.

"Where did this come from? Is someone celebrating a birthday?" Garret asked.

"Uhmm, did I miss something?" Jorge questioned, thinking he had forgotten Eirwen's birthday.

"No, it's just a small celebration for our fifth anniversary since we started assembling the portal. We are more than halfway done. I thought we should have cake," Zillah said with a glowing smile.

"Wait a minute, you're not pregnant again, are you?" Garret asked jokingly. They both quickly denied any further offspring with a shake of their heads before reaching for Zillah's interpretation of a German chocolate cake.

Most of their days were filled with testing portions of the portal. They checked connectivity, power settings, and how the equipment functioned. In this aspect, the mission was comparable to the colonization of Mars. A piece at a time was built independently until they all came together to form a masterpiece. It took many years for Zillah to extrapolate plans and theories from individuals scattered through history. The issue was that there could be no collaboration between any of the people that had the hypothesis. Time was the ultimate barrier that stifled the largest goal.

The next day Zillah entered the board room with all the members seated at the table. She quickly recognized Esther leading the table, but the two individuals in the exosuits with burgundy robes had moved up a position. In their place were two more with similar suits, except these were green. They also seemed to be slightly different in their design, with no robes covering their skin like suits. Ms. Hallaway began the conversation, as she most always did, to control the room.

"We brought you here for a progress report. It has been some time since we have spoken. It is nice to see the progress you have made over the years, but we need to make sure you are on track and moving at a faster pace. It seems you have slowed down since having a child," Ms. Hallaway said abruptly and to the point, quite possibly a little impatient. Zillah gathered her thoughts before even making an attempt at answering the director.

"We have been working steadily on the Quarksandrium. The equipment is very precise and can't be rushed. If we make any mistakes, our lives, anyone near the facility, as well as those in the past and future, could be in serious jeopardy if something goes wrong," Zillah said thoughtfully with a steady and precise volume.

"You may be the expert in your field and have the advantage through leniency, but this board already knows the outcome of your pursuit. We will be gracious this round, but you are on a firm timeline. You have five more years to open the Quarksandrium; do not disappoint us," Esther said, finishing the conversation with a firm gesture and an outstretched hand, calling Zillah to action. As the director finished speaking, the doors magically opened, and Zillah took that as her opportunity to leave. It was apparent around the room that the board had been doing some technology upgrades as well.

After leaving Zander's headquarters, and heading back to her office, she played the meeting over in her mind. *Why is it that the members are always different? And why does it seem that those beings are taking over the company?*

"How was the meeting?" Jorge questioned as Zillah walked into the bay area.

"Typical. They want everything faster and done yesterday. We really need to stay on track with this project. I get a weird feeling when I have to go over there," Zillah explained.

"What do you mean? I never got that feeling when I met with them," Jorge said.

"I just get a weird vibe. Sometimes it feels like they know too much, and they look right through me. Either way, we can't compromise on quality. We have to get this right," Zillah said.

A few more years passed, and the project was nearly complete. It was finally to the point of fine-tuning the software and making minor component adjustments. The machine still might not function for a few years, but everything was mostly assembled. The building would continue construction for the next ten to twenty years, but that wouldn't affect the Quarksandrium itself. It would only change the distance that the vibrations traveled, making it more stable and much easier to span time.

The three had been through several trials of powering on the machine. Still, it never wholly initialized or opened the portal. It took so long to construct the building and get every connection right that it was mind-numbing to think of what could be wrong and why it wouldn't complete the cycle.

"Let's power it down and sleep on it for the evening,

it's been a long day, and we're just going in circles at this point. It's time for the semi-annual clean tonight anyway, and we can start fresh tomorrow," Zillah reluctantly advised as they shut the equipment down. It had been a non-stop run to get everything done in the last few years. They knew they were close but couldn't figure out where the issue was or how to find it.

The semi-annual cleaning was scheduled for that evening, and Mr. Collins was training a new recruit on the list of cleaning procedures. Lucas had received a promotion to sanitation director of building seven. He typically directed the crews and wasn't required to do the cleaning himself. Yet he still made it a personal goal to ensure every new employee knew the proper procedures for his building and the company.

Mr. Collins and the new hire, Rylee Jinkins, were leaving the facility services area early in the evening. Rylee pushed the large cart that held a sizable trashcan, cleaners, mops and brooms, and other janitorial items they would need for the building. This part of their trip would only include the inner parts of the building, the outside of the campus was scheduled for two days later.

"You look good in that dark-gray suit, but your shoes don't appear to be standard for what we should be wearing. You'll need to get the proper shoes," Mr. Collins said as they walked down the long hallway.

"I'm sorry, I knew they weren't the right ones. I just haven't got the shipment yet that I ordered. Apparently, there are still shipment hijackings going on throughout the Midwest. I should get them soon, though," Rylee said with an apologetic tone.

"I understand. Just be careful until you get them," he said with an understanding voice.

The two continued down the hall, winding through the maze of hallways that opened up to a long hallway again.

"We'll be starting just up ahead with the office to the left. Zillah is the one who designed this crazy building. It's a beautiful building but a nightmare to navigate and clean. That's her office there," Lucas said, giving Rylee a history lesson.

"This room is pretty straightforward. Like a majority of the other rooms, just empty the cans, dust, and finish with a sweep and mop," Lucas said.

"I think I understand," she said.

They both made quick work of the office Zillah, Jorge, and Garret were stationed in. As they began to sweep, Lucas called to security for assistance.

"Maintenance to security…"

"Security, go ahead…"

"We are finishing Zillah's office and requesting entry into the control room and bay area for the semi-annual cleaning," Mr. Collins said over the communication devices.

"Roger, we'll send someone over."

Mr. Collins and Rylee were closing the door to Zillah's office when they saw the guard walking down the hall toward them.

"How come the cleaning robots can't take care of these rooms?" Rylee asked.

"These three are the most important rooms of this building and the reason it was built. Plus, we had to call security to even get in them. Zillah is rather paranoid at times and micromanages this part of her job," Mr. Collins explained.

"Evening, sir. We hate to bother you, but we can't get into these two rooms without security clearance for the semi-annual cleaning," Mr. Collins said.

"It's quite alright. I'm used to it. Apparently, the scientists only allow us to swipe in for this one event. Usually, we aren't even allowed in here," the guard said.

"That's pretty crazy," Rylee said.

They entered and cleaned as the guard held the door for them. The control room was reasonably clean, but they continued through the systematic pattern of cleaning the room. The guard pulled the door closed after they finished mopping and ensured the door wouldn't open.

"So, you all must be busy this time of year with all the cleaning?" the guard questioned.

"We have it on a rotation, actually. Tonight, we're cleaning these three rooms and the farms above, then our regular rounds. There's enough throughout the building to keep a six-month cycle on everything. This is Rylee's first night, plus I'm the only one from janitorial services allowed to supervise the cleaning of these two rooms," Mr. Collins explained.

"That's interesting," the guard said as he opened the door to the bay area.

"OK, Rylee, this is a sensitive room. There isn't anything to dust but the workstations scattered around the room. Make sure not to touch any of the tarps covering the equipment in the middle of the room," Lucas said, giving strict instructions.

"I can handle that," she replied.

"After we finish that, we'll sweep and mop," he said.

They made quick work of the dusting and trash cans. Mr. Collins picked up the large items that were left on the floor. Various cable sheathing and other debris littered the floor around the room.

"I'll start sweeping, then you can follow me with a mop. It looks like the scientist raised all the cables off the floor, so there shouldn't be any concern about getting anything on the floor wet. We'll start in the back and work our way toward the door," he continued as they prepared to clean the floor.

Mr. Collins swept the pieces of wire, screws, dust, hair, and solder into piles to collect before mopping. It was crazy how much debris accumulated over six months. Rylee had mopped a majority of the floor behind Mr. Collins as he swept. They were finishing up the last section of the room that contained the racks of servers and various equipment.

"I think we're just about done, Rylee. I know this room can be tough because it's so large," he said, letting out a sigh, as he was getting tired and ready to finish with the cleaning.

Rylee continued behind a rack when suddenly, there was a loud crashing noise.

"Hey, what was that?" The guard yelled from the doorway.

Mr. Collins quickly shuffled over to see what had happened.

"Are you OK? What happened?" Mr. Collins asked.

"I'm OK. My shoes must have slipped on the wet floor while I was mopping. My knee does hurt, though," Rylee said as she leaned up against one of the racks.

"I knew those shoes would be trouble," he said, shaking his head.

"OK, well, let's finish this room so we can get out of here. I'll have to write up a report about your fall, just to cover the bases," Mr. Collins said.

Rylee agreed, and he helped her get up off the ground before walking to talk to the guard. When Rylee looked behind her, she noticed that she must have landed against one of the units. Quickly, Rylee mopped the area and moved closer to the door. She continued to think about the machine she damaged and finally submitted to her guilt.

"Mr. Collins, do you mind if I go clean my knee up? I think it might be bleeding. I'm sorry," Rylee said with a pouting face and a grimace.

"That's fine. I'll finish this area. Meet me back at our office," Mr. Collins said with a sad but understanding look.

Rylee limped off toward the door until she turned the corner and thought the guard couldn't see her anymore, then gained speed as she quickly walked down the hall away from what had happened. As Mr. Collins finished the bay area and stepped into the hall, the guard took a quick look around the room before closed the door.

"Don't be too hard on the girl. It was just an accident. I'm sure nothing was hurt except her pride," the guard said, trying to help Rylee.

"You're probably right. I should have been mopping anyway, since she didn't have the proper shoes," Mr. Collins said.

"I'm glad you all got it done so quickly. It's almost lunchtime, and I'm pretty hungry," the guard commented as they left the area.

"Not a problem. I'll let you know how everything turns out. Hopefully, we'll see you next time," Mr. Collins said to the guard as he shook his hand and left the area.

The next morning, Zillah was running late from dealing with one of Eirwen's crises at home. Jorge and Garret had already uncovered the equipment as they usually would after a cleaning. Both Jorge and Garret were working on verifying the portal's connections. They were still somewhat tired from a long exhausting week. It was most likely the high pressure from Zander and the changes that often occurred that kept them from sleeping well recently. Zillah finally strolled in the room, humming a song she had heard Eirwen practicing for a school musical.

"Good morning, everyone," Zillah said cheerfully, greeting the crew.

Shortly after, a couple of grumbles and eye-rolls ensued. Needless to say, not everyone was having the best morning. As they gathered in the control room, Zillah began going over the startup sequence for a morning run of the equipment.

"Bring up the primary instruments..." Zillah started with a funny accent.

As they brought up the instruments, this was the incident that began their journeys to the past. The fan cage that Rylee had fallen against had smashed against one of the boards, cascading the events they would encounter next. For the first time in all its glorious wonder, the time portal opened up, amazing all those who witnessed it that day. When they shut down the device and investigated, they found the damaged computer cage and fan carnage that brought it together by complete chance. In the days following, they reconfigured the damaged unit and redesigned the circuit boards. Shortly after, they prepared for a second run of the device.

CROSSING OVER

In the weeks following the repair, they discovered the portal would stay open for only three minutes until it crossed out of the time shadow's path. Three minutes wasn't long, but it was a constant they couldn't change. That three minutes would prove to be plenty of time to validate the historical time they had shadowed. They knew the general proximity where the portal would open, since overlaps were finite and ripping time didn't require extended navigation in the project's early stages. It wasn't clear initially what had caused the portal to open outside the intended shadow. Still, the anomaly that allowed them to travel beyond the current decade was a considerable boost to their ego. It validated that the machine was exactly what they needed, to go anywhere in time. Zillah and her team had even beat the expected deadline they were given by the board.

Although the team created the incredible machine, it wasn't truly the Quarksandrium until after returning from *the journey*. Shortly after returning from their trip to Missouri, Jorge was admitted to the hospital for surgery to clean his leg and check his health.

"Hello, you must be Mr. Ruthven. Your doctor called, we've been expecting you," a nurse in the emergency room said to Jorge.

"Yes, I am. Did my leg give it away?" Jorge said, trying to be funny.

"Here, sit down in the chair. This will take you to the exam room, where they will prepare you for surgery. We must get this taken care of quickly. Ma'am, you are welcome to stay in the waiting room, or you can come back later, but no visitors until after his surgery. I have strict instructions from his doctor," the nurse said.

"OK, I understand. I'll check on you later, Jorge, to make sure everything is going well. I'll be at the office. You'll be OK. I love you," Zillah said with a confident reassurance.

The nurse programmed the chair to take him to the exam room, and he hovered away as Zillah walked back to building seven. Even though Goramaius had given him a shot to prevent the infection, he was still suffering and needed significant medical attention.

"Mr. Ruthven, I have looked over your chart and blood work. You will need an operation to clean the wound, cut out the affected areas, and close it up. It looks like you were given some sort of virus inhibitor, but it's one I've never seen before. One of the nurses will be back shortly to help you get ready for surgery," the doctor said.

As the nurse prepared Jorge for surgery on his leg, he sent his wife a text to advise her what was going on. *They are preparing me for surgery to clean and repair the wound. I'll message you when I get out, probably in a few hours.* It turned out that tainted dirt had got in the wound and farther in his leg than they initially considered. The surgeons cleaned the injury and leg the best they could, but there was already permanent damage, and it was thought that he would have a limp the rest of his life.

While Jorge was getting medical treatment, Zillah worked with Garret to integrate the orb into the portal's center. It was strange how all the random pieces fit together sometimes, almost like it was preordained. They opened the polyhedron-shaped container in the center of the machine. The twenty-eight-sided globe had a hallow cavity in the center that would fit the dimensions of the orb they retrieved from Goramaius. Zillah and Garret removed several of the triangle plates and support arms from the front of the polyhedron to gain access to its cavity.

"Why won't it fit?" Zillah said as she began to get frustrated.

She set the abnormal sphere back down on a nearby table to inspect the space again. Looking all around the cavity where the relic was intended to fit, she found a coin similar to the one they had given Goramaius. It was wedged near the top of the space out of sight.

"Great! Well, since I am being open now, it appears

there's another relic in here that I didn't notice before we left. Surely, I would have noticed it earlier if it had been here, but it's in a weird place. Maybe I missed it. And before you say it, I didn't tell Jorge about it either before we left. I suppose it will all come out eventually anyway," Zillah said.

"Well, it was kind of hidden up there, but with all the weird stuff that's been happening lately..." Garret began, then lowered his voice to a whisper.

"...we can't rule out that someone put it there after you left. And, it's OK, I know you have to keep some things from me," he said.

Zillah thought for a minute, pondering Garret's suggestion.

"True, some of these things do seem awfully coincidental at times. I don't intentionally leave everyone in the dark. It's just I'm not sure everyone needs to know every detail."

The amulet was about four inches across but no more than one-quarter inch thick. Was it a coincidence that it was the same size as the medallion they had given Goramaius in exchange for the Quarksandrium orb? It even had a similar inscription and symbols around the outer edge. Was it actually the same one or a different one?

Zillah didn't say anything to Garret about the medallion they gave to Goramaius. After the medallion was removed, the globe fit snugly inside, completing the Quarksandrium. Zillah didn't remember making this part of the hole to any specific dimensions. However, it was a perfect fit. She paused for a moment and thinking of Garret's words about coincidences. *Was it fate? Did someone manipulate the schematics?* Some things that happened were just too ironic to be fate.

After reassembling the portal again, Zillah returned to Jorge at the hospital, recovering from his surgery. He would be there another day before he would be on his feet again. Although it was just a preventive surgery to keep the disease from spreading, it was still invasive and intense. They wouldn't know the exact ramifications of the incident until years later. She opened the door to his room and peeked in. He was still resting, but she quietly entered anyway and sat in a chair near the bed.

"Zillah, you're here?" Jorge mumbled as he woke up.

"Yes, I'm here. How are you feeling?" she said with a soft voice.

"Tired," he replied. She looked at him, holding his hand.

"Just rest, love," she said as he closed his eyes and drifted back to sleep.

"You're still here," he said later as he woke again.

"Of course, I'm still here. I do have something to tell you, though," she said lovingly, looking into his eyes. She reached in her pocket and pulled out the medallion.

"Where did you get that? It looks like the one we

gave Goramaius," he said with a puzzled look on his face while he began to sit up.

"It does look that way, doesn't it? It was in the portal's center. We suspected the pyramid changed our trajectory, taking us to the snow highway, but the coin must have had some kind of effect, too. It had to have warped the time coordinates, don't you think? We need more data to figure it out. I know the Quarksandrium was supposed to help us, but I didn't realize I had designed the orb to fit it exactly. I need to update some of the portal's programming. Do you mind if I go take care of that while you're here? Then we can test and get the data we need. I don't want to get the board involved again," she said quickly, anticipating Jorge wouldn't want her to leave.

"Go on and do what you need to. I will be getting out of here tomorrow, and we can go from there," he said, still half dazed but granting her comfort that she didn't have to stay with him. She kissed him, shoved the amulet back in her pocket.

When she arrived back at her office, she immediately began changing the parameters to allow any historical date when shadowing jumping. Before adding the orb relic, the machine was programmed to only allow shadowing in the previous decade. Her hope was that with the orb, they could travel beyond the decade restriction. It took her the rest of the night and into the morning to remove the safeguards they had put in place.

As the clock rolled through the morning hours, Zillah finally completed all the programming to allow for expanded time travel. As she saved her work, she realized it was nearly noon. She had been expecting Garret to come in, which would let her know it was about eight or nine in the morning. She forgot it was Saturday, and she needed to get back to the hospital to accompany Jorge home. In a panic about how late it was, Zillah hoped he hadn't left the hospital already. She picked up her phone and sent a quick message. *I'm so sorry, I'll be there in twenty minutes. Sorry, I lost track of time.* She didn't wait for a reply. She put her suit on and headed for the door. As she was about to put her helmet on, she received a return text from Jorge. *It's OK, they are just finishing up the paperwork, and I expect an exit consult about the time you get here. See you soon.*

Zillah made her way to the hospital entrance. As she made her way back to the second floor, she passed a gift machine. The thought a cheap gift wasn't exactly her style, but feeling guilty for being late, she stopped and pressed a few buttons. The device immediately picked up her suit's electronic signature. It paid for the transaction as the greeting card she had selected dropped into the bin. She was in such a hurry, she forgot to remove her helmet. Pressing the button sequence on her forearm, the helmet released, and she attached it to her hip before retrieving the card. She looked around and found a pen on a counter nearby to sign the card. The greeting card was pale blue on the front with a picture of balloons. She opened the card to write a quick word and noticed the inscription. *Congratulations on your new baby boy.* She hadn't paid attention to the description on the machine before she made the rushed purchase.

She closed her eyes and shook her head. It was just one of those days, I guess. After a bit of consideration, she wrote: *My Love, I know you will endure. God didn't put us here to be weak. I'm glad to be fulfilling my destiny with you. PS sorry about the card, we're not pregnant.* She sealed up the envelope and wrote *Jorge* on the front of it. Zillah turned the corner into the hospital room where Jorge was sitting on the bed.

"Here she is now," Jorge said to the nurse.

"OK, I will get the last of your paperwork ready, and the doctor will be in shortly," the nurse said.

"What did she say?" Zillah questioned.

"That was about the extent of it. I really don't know much yet. It's been rather strange. The doctors haven't said much about anything," Jorge replied.

"Here, I got you a card," she said as she handed him the card. He opened the card and chuckled as he read it.

"Thank you, that was kind of typical for this journey, I suppose," he said with a half-smile.

The doctor entered the room with a familiar scroll computer containing Jorge's information.

"Hello Mr. Ruthven, I hope you are feeling well.

The surgery went well, and you're clear to go home. We cleaned the wound, and it should heal nicely. Unfortunately, you may have some permanent muscle damage to the area and a limited range of motion. I have put a referral in for physical therapy. The equipment for it should be shipped to your home in a few days. We removed all the waste and debris from your leg, but we still need to monitor that it didn't enter the bloodstream and cause any other damage. You will need another test in three months and annually after that. Do you have any questions?" the doctor said with a slow and steady voice.

"I don't understand. Does that mean I am in the clear? How can you not be sure if there are still traces of toxins from the air?" Jorge asked, not fully believing what he was hearing.

"There is no evidence in your blood or around the wound that we saw, but traces could have already traveled inside your body that we didn't detect. We are just being cautious. Follow your rehabilitation schedule, and we'll schedule a follow-up. I wish you a speedy recovery," the doctor said as he turned and left the room.

"Well, all we can do is enjoy what we have right now. We were never guaranteed tomorrow. Let's get going. I'm exhausted," Zillah said, giving Jorge her best "attaboy" speech.

Jorge hobbled to the transport chair and sat down. It looked like a very basic recliner, except that there was a keypad on the arm. The nurse entered the room and pushed the navigation buttons on the chair, programming its destination. She handed the exit paperwork to Zillah and wished them a good afternoon before pushing the chair's enter command.

"Your transportation vehicle is waiting downstairs to take you home," the nurse said.

The lights under the chair began to glow when the chair started to levitate, stabilizing into a hover a few inches above the ground. As it began moving toward the elevator, Zillah followed along beside her husband. The elevator quickly reached the lower level, where there was a garage entrance. Almost seamlessly, the chair began to move again toward the front of the building where a vehicle was waiting.

It was a small two-person transport vehicle. As with most inner-city cars, it was a hybrid vehicle derived from power sources after the Quenomoly, yet it had a classic electric car sound. All transport vehicles went through the garage since it had chambered entrance and exit areas for all vehicles, exchanging toxic air for breathable air. Most cars were driverless and relied on identification chips either in a person's suite or communication device.

"Destination, 3013 Browning Avenue," Jorge advised the car.

"Thank you... Payment received. Enjoy your trip, Zander Enterprises," the car said.

Even though walking tubes were common

throughout the city, houses still had compression bays near the street to accommodate longer distances and assisted transportation that guests often used. Nearly all the vehicles were automated, except for those people who had government clearance for extended travel.

As the car cleared the bay and the green light came on to exit the vehicle, the sun was setting, and Jorge paused. He was perched on his crutches, ready to go to the house, when he was struck by the sun's beauty. He stopped to feel the fleeting warmth of the sunshine through the dirt-spotted glass. Most of the time, they wouldn't risk having their helmet off until they returned indoors, but Jorge felt like time was limited, and he wanted to enjoy the moment. Even through the contaminated air, there was something magnificent about a beautiful setting sun.

"Sometimes, there just are no words," Jorge muttered under his breath.

"What's that?" Zillah questioned.

"Nothing, dear, I'm just glad to be home," he replied contentedly.

Zillah helped Jorge through his therapy the next few nights using the various equipment to help the wound heal and his muscles regain strength. Before they could blink, it was Monday. They were back in the office talking about the plan to move forward with the Quarksandrium testing and gathering more data.

The next few trips back through time were very

interesting to Zillah. The first few trips would be easily confirmable by witnessing events that happened on the day they expected to shadow. Large catastrophes and wars were the easiest to recognize, since they were documented most thoroughly throughout time. They chose September eleventh 2001 as their first destination. It would be easy to distinguish the time of day and location.

"I believe we're ready. I have the time set for nine fifty-eight a.m. At least there shouldn't be any aircraft flying to interrupt the portal opening," Garret said as he prepared the settings of the portal for operation.

"I have to say, I'm a little nervous about this one. Watching the south tower fall of the World Trade Center seems kind of morbid," Jorge said.

"It's either that or watch a battle from the Civil War. I thought this would be the lesser of the two," Zillah said as they continued preparing for the mission.

"Why can't we just pick something fun? Like the Olympics or something," Jorge asked.

"It would be harder to discern an ordinary crowd gathering. That could happen literally anywhere," Zillah exclaimed.

The location wasn't based on typical longitude, latitude, and elevation historically used to find a position on Earth. Instead, it used a variation of space measurement. The Earth's current position was always "moment zero"; it calculated where the Earth would have been at a particular time in history. The marked coordinates were in reference to the universe instead of the sun. It allowed for a broader range of historical targets they typically wouldn't have had by only using Earth's coordinates alone.

The mission was to observe the building from a distance. The intent wasn't to watch the people or gain clarity about the situation, but to witness the building as it fell, almost like an ordinary building being demolished. They set the Quarksandrium's guidance systems to the correct historical time and coordinates.

The power-up sequence went as usual compared to previous similar missions. Garret, Jorge, and Zillah would call signals to each other as they powered the machine and initiated the core sequence. It was extraordinary to think they could see a live representation or a personally recorded video of historical events. Ravyn once again operated the robotic arm. It pushed through the portal and rested for just over two minutes before she retracted it. They couldn't remember if it seemed like an eternity or a blink of an eye, but time continued at the same pace it always had, one second at a time.

The camera emerged from the portal, smoking and covered in dust. The team wasn't sure what to make of the discovery. Garret wiped the dust off the recorder as the smell of ash filled the bay area. It took only a moment to upload the footage to their computers. What the three would see next would be unimaginable and something they would never forget.

A large smoking building was reduced to rubble in a matter of seconds. The sounds were haunting, even though they weren't actually there. The building let out sounds of creaking, popping, and other unexplainable sounds. People were screaming as they ran or fell from high floors into the rubble below. Tears rolled down Zillah's face, considering what those people went through, and all people through time who have had such considerable tragedy affect their lives. It made her think of the Quenomoly and all the people who suffered, eventually dying from that event. It was over-whelming, yet they still hadn't found a way to avoid any of it.

The time navigation was accurate, but the footage of events was supposed to be much farther away. After reviewing the footage, the three discovered the portal was several hundred feet from where it was supposed to open. Judging by the footage, they were very close to the historic terrorist attack on the twin towers. The camera must have been close enough to the building debris to have a layer of dust accumulated all over the unit.

It was such a monumental day for them, yet they still had heavy hearts and felt sad. Sometimes words can't describe what images and emotions in the actual moment can bring to a situation. They sat quietly for a while without saying a word to each other. Sometimes the first occurrence of an event in our lives takes on a new meaning, and it was hard for them to express what they were thinking.

This would be the first mission of the completed Quarksandrium, but there were many more to accomplish their ultimate goal. The team truly believed they could change the outcome of the Quenomoly and revert time, even if it meant they would never exist in the altered timeline.

CIRCLES

Admittedly, sticking a camera through a tear in time isn't the best idea, to go unnoticed by previous generations. It could cause quite a few issues if someone were to see something like this happen. Zillah held a meeting in a nearby conference room with all the crew.

"First of all, I want to say congratulations to Ravyn for being hired full-time," Zillah said as everyone clapped.

"With that said, we need to continue pushing the boundaries of the timelines and what the Quarksandrium can do. We need an alternate way of surveilling the past that allows us to somewhat control our detection. Does anyone have any suggestions?" Zillah asked.

"What about rovers or an all-terrain vehicle?" Ravyn asked.

"I don't think that would be good. What if the portal has another error and the opening isn't where it's expected to be? The rover would fall to Earth and be destroyed, but we'd be leaving our technology in the past. That wouldn't be good at all," Jorge said.

"Valid point," Ravyn agreed.

"How about a fly or bug that is equipped with cameras? Don't you have a friend that works with those, Zillah?" Garret asked.

"Well, that won't work. What if it needs to cross a considerable distance? The smaller the robot, the longer it would take to get to where it needed to be, and it may run out of power," Ravyn said with a snarky tone, since her idea was shot down.

"We can't have a huge monster aircraft; that would be noticed too quickly. We could do period-correct aircraft, but then again, it wouldn't be cost-effective to create an aircraft for every time we want to go back in time," Jorge said, shooting down his own idea.

"In researching events throughout the past, we've encountered many stories of UFOs. How about we use some of those designs to create a drone?" Zillah suggested.

"I guess that's why you're the boss. You have all the ideas," Garret quickly said.

Drones did seem like the logical answer to the dilemma. They decided that a crewless aircraft would be the least invasive but provide the agility they needed. It would also be easier to maneuver out of sight, and they could dispose of them in areas that were thought to be undiscovered. Many of the first drones were programmed to be scuttled in the depths of the ocean to avoid being discovered. Sometimes it wasn't easy to recover the crafts they sent back, but the information they received from looking at historic articles would be the critical information they needed to continue.

Early drones were not huge; they were about three feet in diameter. They were much smaller drones than the ones which would succeed them. Since they were also limited by the ground they could cover, operating in the night hours was critical. Should the portal's arrival time be off, light sensors on the drone would assess the sun's position to determine if it needed to wait or terminate the mission. A few drones required self-destruction sequences to be made over nearby bodies of water. A unique onboard guidance system navigated the ship off-grid in a non-technical world. Tiny cameras and other sensors were mounted in the drone to log additional historical information. The onboard technology also allowed the craft to find suitable targets for tagging.

Zander seemed to anticipate that the project would need a sizable number of drones to accomplish the goals ahead. A year after the first drones flew, a division was created that designed and built drones for Zillah's team. Although the drone teams didn't know the drone's exact purpose, they did know that Zillah and her team used the craft for exploration and scientific research. Innovation and further development continued to expand the ships' abilities as they received feedback from the missions.

Zillah's team's primary goal was to reliably fine-tune

the arrival time and position of the Quarksandrium. The quickest way to accomplish this was to design pre-configured flight patterns in the drones they sent back. Not only would this work in a nontechnical world, but it would allow the team to venture farther back in time. The farther back in time they traveled, the more significant the margin of error seemed to be.

Garret set the destination time to late in the twentieth century, when the portal would deliver the small drone in an area of South America. The drone was designed to include all the hardware necessary to navigate and gather the information required for future missions.

The drone used for this mission was spherical in shape, typically what people would call a UFO. Disguising the drone as an alien ship was the most logical and dismissive idea to utilize. It was expected that people in the past would perceive the craft to be alien technology because they had no idea what the future held. It was far beyond technology their minds could comprehend.

With the lack of GPS in those days, the ship used multiple onboard guidance systems. It was also equipped with cameras that would search for the nearest crops. After finding a notable crop, the drone would quickly descend within a few feet of the ground. It moved in symmetrical patterns while systematically laying parts of the crops down, making designs later called crop circles. Such an incredible phenomenon would be documented by farm owners. The team could retrieve historical documents when these occurrences happened and calibrate the portal's timing and location.

A month had passed since they sent the drone to South America. After expanding their search globally, they found the device's location in Europe. It turned out that the nearest town was called Parlin, in Poland, where the drone descended that night. Even though it had required significant search time, they found evidence in history matching the drone's programming design.

It was briefly after that they gathered in the center of building number seven with Esther to commemorate the event by naming the building after the small town. As Esther removed the cloth from a small plaque, she gave a short speech.

"We are here to memorialize this historical moment, which only a few will be thoroughly knowledgeable about, named after a small town that has given us historical guidance to achieve insurmountable things in this great world. In this building, we begin pursuing great things in the future and the past. With that, we name this building 'Parlin Center.' Thank you all for your hard work," Esther said as the crowd began to clap.

Soon after the ceremony, they recalibrated the machine and began making other trips worldwide. They continued fine-tuning the instruments on the

Quarksandrium with many crop circle missions. Generally, the circles they designed were referenced to the Parlin Center, which Zillah had architected. The patterns varied in each location. Still, they had some sort of similarity that reflected the Parlin Center's annual layout. These markers helped them confirm the coordinates and time in history that they explored.

"Hello," Harold said, answering the phone.

"Hi, Harold. We're preparing to expand our capabilities with the drones in the next couple of years," Zillah said.

"Do you have anything in particular in mind? What are the objectives?" he began asking.

"I'll leave that to you. The base model is working well for atmospheric conditions. Still, we ultimately need better awareness, recording ability, and a variety of camera views would be a great start. Now that I'm thinking about it, enhanced stealth ability would be nice," Zillah said.

"That sounds doable. We're working on some other things too, but we can tweak those along the way," Harold noted.

It wasn't long before the drone division made massive enhancements to the primitive ship design. The drone team was continually adding new technology to navigate and gather information from its surroundings, including variables such as atmospheric conditions and multiple reconnaissance imaging. They began to change the ship's size and shape throughout numerous missions to find what worked best. However, some of these designs were not without significant adversity. Among the top failures in the structures was the cigar drone. It was reported multiple times in history before completing its mission and was quickly scrapped.

Advances in drone navigation and propulsion were at the top of the list for enhancements. Multiple clocks and the ability to adjust between times were also of concern. Some of these patterns were easier to adjust once they had the Quarksandrium's timelines tuned. The possibilities were endless, but they quickly focused on circular and triangular crafts with smooth rounded edges for testing.

"Well, it's taken five years since we received the primary relic, but we finally have the Quarksandrium tuned, and we understand our timeline trajectory. This large hangar doesn't do us much good if the portal is small. We need to redesign the portal to accommodate the new drones' larger size," Zillah said to the crew gathered inside the bay area.

"That sounds like fun," Garret said as he smirked.

"At least we'll be able to utilize a larger size of the bay area," Jorge said.

"How big are we talking about?" Ravyn asked.

"Twenty yards wide should be enough. I expect this expansion phase to take another couple of years. The new set of drones will cover more ground and mark time more quickly after building the new portal. During the portal expansion, we will also upgrade equipment and condense technology where possible. It won't be an easy task," Zillah said with fortitude.

"Does that mean we'll finally be able to use the ceiling hangar doors?" Ravyn asked.

"Yes, and air cycle units we haven't used yet for the hangar," Zillah replied.

The team worked together over the next several years through the demolition and reconstruction of the new portal. The Quarksandrium and the housing that embraced the relic stayed the same size. However, the edge that contained the orb's dark matter was much more extensive. The hangar was about the size of a football field, yet the portal would be much smaller.

Before they rebuilt the launch pad, they would dispose of the crafts in the ocean or large water bodies that were still intact in the future. Of course, self-destruction was always a possibility, but not the preferred method. It was messy and had unknown consequences, as they found out in Roswell, which was not far from them. Because of the earlier craft's smaller size and limited speed, they usually picked somewhere close to where the circles would be drawn when getting rid of the ships.

The new team's drones were much larger crafts that would be able to traverse the globe. It was even possible to navigate underwater. Ships' cameras could self-identify nearly any item and establish the distance it was from the craft. The ships could also identify the density and temperature of the objects.

The new ships were self-aware objects that were explicitly programmed for recognizance missions. They were also extremely lightweight, made from ore returned from the comet strike during the Quenomoly. The new drones were also propelled with the same energy-drive technology that allowed such quick movements of vehicles after the comet.

The team found that the farther back in time they went, the harder it was to locate the events' documentation because of the scarcity of reporting and documentation. They always knew they couldn't rely on reports of miscellaneous aircraft flying or field patterns being found in new articles. It was an easier way to document history without having to stash a futuristic aircraft in thoughtful places.

The team was setting up for their first mission with one of the new drones.

"The systems are coming online," Garret said as he initiated the sequences for launch.

"… I…. can't…" Jorge began to speak but was having trouble getting the words out. Gasping for air, he clenched his throat and chest.

"Shut it down!" Garret yelled to everyone just before they all ran to Jorge. Zillah hit the emergency distress connection on her phone to request help. Jorge was in serious need of medical attention. It was convenient that the hospital had a large drone available to shuttle Zillah and Jorge to the hospital from the building's roof. Many medical types of transport used drone technology to expedite transportation in emergency scenarios.

"You're going to be OK," Zillah said frantically to Jorge. Deep inside, her anxiety was through the roof with concern. They closed the doors, and the drone lifted off. It took only about five minutes to get between buildings. It took longer for the team to get Jorge's helmet on and out of the elevator on the roof than it took for the drone to get to the hospital.

Upon arrival, medical personnel worked on Jorge, restoring his oxygen levels to a normal range. After working with Jorge in the emergency room for what seemed like hours, they moved him and Zillah to the fourth floor for observation and more tests. It appeared that the more serious the issue got, the farther away from the ground floor he traveled to recover.

A steady flow of nurses checked on Jorge when he initially got to his hospital room. They took blood, checked vitals, and made the casual small talk in attempts to divert his attention to something other than what they were doing. The next day a new doctor came in to speak with them.

"Well, the good news is you're still with us," the doctor said, trying to be positive. "Unfortunately, it seems the accident you had several years ago has traveled to your lungs, and there's no way to reverse it. You'll need to carry an oxygen supply with you from now on. I'll admit you don't have an easy road ahead. Cases like this typically don't fare well over the long haul," the doctor said with remorse in his voice.

"Are you saying I don't have long to live, Doctor?" Jorge asked.

"None of us have a date stamped on us, Jorge. I can't say for certain how long you will live. However, many cases such as yours are shorter than a decade. We will do the best to help you stay around as long as possible, but there is no cure for this. I'm sorry. I will come back in a while and check on you and see if you have any questions after we go over your treatments," the doctor said, continuing to console him.

As he turned to leave the room, Zillah and Jorge blankly stared at each other in disbelief. There were no words that could undo what they just heard. It was a decisive blow right in their stomach that yanked the air out of both of them. Fear and sadness were the most substantial feelings, in the beginning. Zillah held Jorge's hand as they sat silently with each other.

Jorge fought the flood of thoughts and feelings that came storming into his mind. *How and why is this happening to me? How will Zillah and Eirwen cope with me being gone?* The number of questions he had seemed to be enormous. He was paralyzed with emotion and numb to everything around him as he continued thinking. *What could I do now to make sure they are taken care of when I'm gone or is it too late to plan for my exit?*

They were often so wrapped up in work that they forgot to enjoy the simple things. Eirwen had been dating off and on. He wondered if he would be around to even give her away when the time came or even a chance to see his grandbabies. Sometimes it was just too much to think about. Zillah had similar thoughts. She thought of the times they would miss eating together or playing cards. Then her mind drifted to when they worked together on projects as a team and came up with incredible ideas and strategies that nobody else could have comprehended.

A nurse walked into Jorge's room after the doctor consulted with him.

"I bet you weren't expecting to be here three days when you got here. I'm sure you'll be glad to get out of here. Here's the list of directions the doctor talked with you about. A list of medications and when to take them is in here. We're also sending you home with an oxygen machine. The doctor suggests resting for a few weeks before returning to work," the nurse said.

Zillah continued to prepare the missions and work while Jorge was recovering at home. It helped her mind stay busy and not focus on the time she would lose with Jorge, not realizing that the time she spent on projects was, in reality, taking away from her time with him. It still wasn't avoidable, since they needed a way to cover medical costs and retain Zander's medical benefits.

A couple of weeks after the hospital visit, Jorge returned to work feeling better than when he had left. Medicine was a miraculous thing, but he knew it wasn't enough to conquer death. It was inevitable, since he was only human after all, even though sometimes the supernatural seemed to surround them every day. It appeared those things were taken for granted sometimes since they became "normal" everyday events. Everything loses its luster over time and needs a renewing of enthusiasm. Maybe Jorge getting sick was the grounding they both needed to have a more fulfilled life.

Shortly after Jorge returned to his regular work routine, the team worked on the drone in preparation for the next day's voyage. They had a pretty steady cycle of programming the drone, sending it back in time, and retrieving it from the mountain range a few hours away. There were several different drone types they maneuvered on these missions. Some were long-range, and some were domestic. Up to this point, all were within Earth's atmosphere, to remain efficient as possible.

Zillah was connected to the drone with a tablet in the bay area, uploading directions and coordinates for the mission, when Garret made the call over the communication devices.

"I'm going to do some low-level testing of the portal. It won't be completely powered up, but I need to check the configurations," Garret said.

"That should be fine. I'm a safe distance away," Zillah said in return.

Garret was essentially going through a checklist of standard operational settings they observed before opening the portal. This time was different, since Zillah had the medallion relic in her pocket. It must have been close enough to the portal that it reacted and began to glow through her pocket. It was a majestic hue that pulsed and cycled around the surface of the sizable coin-shaped relic.

Zillah's eyes widened as she realized her mouth was hanging open; then she closed it, hoping nobody had seen her. As she began to smirk, her eyes brightened, and an unthinkable idea came to her as she yelled to Jorge and Garret.

"HEY! Jorge and Garret, get over here," she hollered through the communication device to the two of them. Garret saw Jorge jog over to Zillah in the launch room, losing his breath along the way.

"Everything OK in there?" Garret said on the intercom.

"Yes, leave everything as it is and come in here, quick!" Zillah said with urgency.

"What are you two looking at?" Garret asked as he joined the two huddled at the drone.

"Look at this. It started glowing when you turned the Quarksandrium on to do testing," Zillah exclaimed.

"What is it? Wait, is that the relic you had before?" Garret asked with a puzzled look on his face.

"Yes, it's Parmathian. It must have a connection to the Quarksandrium like it did the pyramid," Jorge said as he looked over out of the corner of his eye as he put the pieces together in his mind.

"Wait, what pyramid? I knew about the coin, but not about the pyramid," Garret questioned.

"It was beginning to get complicated with the travel and board members being demanding. We just didn't know what it meant at the time," Zillah answered.

"This could be a huge breakthrough, but you all are keeping me out of the loop. I know I'm part of the team, but I can't help if you keep me in the dark," Garret said as he closed his eyes, then squinted with frustration before turning, walking toward the door.

"Well, that didn't go well, but I guess he's right. We should have given him the whole story," Jorge said.

"We'll just have to do better at communicating next time. Garret is usually pretty mellow. He'll get over it," Zillah said flippantly.

"I'm not sure time is on our side, Zillah," Jorge said as he went back to the electronic cabinet he was working on in the corner. For some reason, the mood changed after that. The rest of the day, they worked in their separate spaces on the project. Zillah hadn't even thought to enlighten Ravyn about the situation, which was part of the problem with her thought process.

They hadn't really figured out what it meant when the trinket was glowing while the unit was turned on. It occasionally crossed their minds about the incident that caused the friction between them. Still, they mostly let it go and never talked about it again.

A few weeks later, Garret came in with a large smile on his face. Zillah and Jorge were sitting at the consoles, looking over charts and settings.

"I just had an incredible idea. What if we could control the drone with the relic through time? Do you think the medallion is linked in a way we can send back information to the Quarksandrium?" Garret asked the group with excitement. The idea immediately sent chills through Zillah. Jorge's eyes got wide, and Ravyn nodded her head.

"That literally just sent chills up my arms! That is an amazing idea," Zillah said. "Let's begin to test that theory," she remarked.

The following days, the four immediately began designing the internal structure and connections for the drone's command unit. Zillah received a new concept drone from the drone division for a new Ultra-rapid Featherweight Organometallic drone. They immediately began to modify the specifications of the new drone.

"Hi Harold, it's Zillah," Zillah began as she called Harold about the drone.

"Hey, Zillah," Harold replied.

"I love the new drone's capabilities, but I've made some modifications that we want to try on the next mission. Can you accommodate those changes before you send them over?" Zillah said with excitement.

"I'll have a look, but it shouldn't be an issue. I'm sure your changes are thorough," Harold said.

The newly designed UFO would have a position for the coin-shaped relic in its heart, and they could control it from any distance or across any time. It would also give live interaction to their current time and allow them to maneuver it appropriately if it made contact with anyone or anything in the past.

The drone teams expected the new project to be delivered within ten months. Unfortunately, Jorge's health wouldn't hold out that long. He deteriorated rapidly over the next six months. He was in and out of the hospital over the next several months, until the stays gradually got longer and longer.

Several more months went by while Jorge went in and out of the hospital, until he eventually never left. They had moved him to the sixth floor with the long-term patients. Zillah still visited him daily, whether she really had the time or not. She felt it was her obligation to be there for him till the very end. Eirwen often visited too, although not as much as her mother. She was busy with school and a new internship with Zander, not to mention she was getting ready for her wedding coming up in the next few months. It was difficult for her, knowing that Jorge might not be able to attend.

His breathing took a toll on his energy levels, and his body struggled to get the oxygen that it needed. The Epsiletacell disease had taken over his lungs and prevented him from recovering in many areas. His muscles began to waste the more he lay in the hospital, gradually losing weight and mass. While Jorge was in the hospital, Zillah continued working on the project, completing bits and pieces with Garret and

Ravyn, running the same simulations as they had in the past.

Zillah and Garret were the only two left on a Friday evening, researching a mission they had completed earlier in the week. During the Quenomoly, nearly half of the information on the internet was damaged and non-recoverable. Large gaps of missing information made it difficult to research their missions. They resorted to various types of computer media that hadn't been used for centuries, such as DVD, Blu-ray disks, and in some cases newspapers on Laserfiche. Combing through the piles of information by hand wasn't easy. However, it was necessary to verify what had changed in history, if anything.

Garret decided to call it a week and head home, leaving Zillah to her work. It was nearly seven on that atypical day when Eirwen called Zillah to let her know Jorge was awake and active that night. It was a memorable night the two shared as Jorge drifted in and out of consciousness while Zillah and Eirwen conversed and played cards. It was one she would never forget.

As the two planes of her dream and reality collided, she woke in a flurry of fright, thinking it was Monday morning. After looking at a clock, she quickly realized it was only Saturday, just before noon. She had recapped the last of their journey in her sleep that started during her conversation with Eirwen the day before.

GOODBYES

After Zillah woke, she pondered a few minutes on the things she dreamt during the night, before gathering her things to head home. She rarely stayed the night, but with the exhaustion and late night with Eirwen, she slept pretty hard as the dreams overwhelmed her. Thankfully it was a weekend, and she didn't have anywhere to be that morning. The nurses came and went a few times to check on Jorge. She finally decided to make her way home and get cleaned up. Grasping Jorge's hand one more time before leaving, she leaned over and kissed him on the forehead until they would meet again.

As the next couple of weeks passed, Jorge's health continued to gradually deteriorate in the hospital. Zillah and Garret continued the tedious process of programming the drones for reconnaissance in the past. They still programmed the occasional crop circle, but not as often as the earlier days.

"Have you heard how the new drones are coming along?" Garret asked Zillah.

QUARKSANDRIUM: THE BEGINNING

"Last I heard, they were still upgrading cameras and working through some last-minute design issues. It will be nice when it finally comes together, and we can insert the relic. I'm just struggling lately with Jorge. I can feel it coming, but I don't want to let go. I'm not sure how I will handle this without him," she said, explaining as her eyes began to well with tears. A sad face grew on Garret as he comforted her.

"He means a lot to us all. This is why we pursue this journey. We need to help those that have been lost or will be lost to these types of infections."

The two separated after a short embrace and went to their desks in silence. The silence was familiar recently, since Jorge wasn't there much anymore. Sometimes it was more the thought of him that was there, even though he hadn't died yet. It was still somber.

The next week, Zillah lost her concentration searching through the archives for a mission they just ran. The combination of a growling belly and a broken heart was just enough to sidetrack her mind. She had that familiar feeling of needing sustenance but didn't have the will or desire to actually eat. As the clock crossed 1:00 p.m., she decided to visit Jorge.

"Garret, I'm going to the hospital," Zillah advised.

He simply nodded his head with understanding as she walked out the door. Zillah went through the usual routine of putting her gear on and following the corridors to exit the building. Sometimes it gave her way too much time to think about everything. The walk between the buildings seemed to get longer and longer as the days went on.

As she arrived on the sixth floor, there was an unusually high number of people moving around. It looked like half of the hall was freshly painted and sectioned off for construction. She didn't ever remember seeing this many people on the sixth floor. Come to think of it, all she ever saw on the floor was nurses that attended to Jorge. Nobody else ever moved around. She began to wonder if there had even been people in the other rooms.

Among the construction workers and nurses, she noticed Jorge's doctor walking toward her.

"What's going on?" she asked him with a concerned look on her face.

"I'm sorry to be the one to tell you this, but Jorge went into an incapacitated state last night. He won't be able to communicate anymore with the outside world, in his condition. I do have some news about an isolated experiment if you are interested in hearing about it," the doctor said, propositioning Zillah.

"What are you talking about? What could possibly help at this point? Why couldn't we have tried this sooner?" she asked with a puzzled look on her face with hints of anxiety, gradually gaining momentum into an angry tone.

"Well, to say it bluntly, it's a hazardous maneuver we would have to undertake. It's not typically given to the public or someone with more than a week of life expectancy. Jorge has been in such high standing with Zander for many years in fulfilling many military contracts that the government was willing to extend the courtesy of this operation. It's not likely he will survive, but there is a chance he could pull through to live a few more years. They are the only ones who have the expertise and resources to accomplish it. The partnership is willing to cover all the procedures without cost to you. It's literally a once-in-a-lifetime opportunity to get a little bit of extra time. A general is here with additional paperwork and information if you decide to continue with the process."

The doctor finished with a caring gesture of one hand behind her elbow, as he turned and went into Jorge's room. Zillah didn't know whether to be happy, angry, or what other emotion could come out of this situation. It was all so overwhelming.

The general turned the corner on the far end of the hallway with four military officers following him, matching his stride and step, as they walked toward Zillah. Their shoes were polished, suits pressed and pristine. The general stopped in front of Zillah, with his hat removed, and extended his hand to greet her.

"You must be Zillah Ruthven. I am General Phillips. I hope the doctor has had enough time to brief you on your husband's situation. Time is not on our side in this situation, and the window to perform this procedure is finite. I understand you have a power of attorney for your husband?" the general questioned.

"I do. This is all a whirlwind. Do you have any more detail I can go on?" she asked, not sure of the situation.

"Mrs. Ruthven, here is a copy of the proceedings and all relevant information that you need to make this decision. We cannot disclose certain information due to the United Earth Secrecy Act of Mars 2287. This document outlines that Mr. Ruthven has, at best, a fifteen percent chance of survival and recovery with a potential of two years beyond that. Without the procedure, he is only expected to live an additional week. As I said, time is finite, and we must act quickly. Please read over the documents. I will return in thirty minutes to collect your signed paperwork if you want to proceed."

One of the general's officers handed him an electronic tablet he retrieved from a briefcase. General Phillips paused, looked down at the device, and reached to place them in Zillah's hands. As quickly as they had come down the hall, they turned and were gone again. Like a well-oiled machine, they seemed to move fluidly and in unison.

Zillah sat down at a nearby table to look over the documents on the device. Thirty minutes wouldn't really allow her to read through all the material. Not to mention, she wasn't even in the right frame of mind to be reading or signing anything. It was out of nowhere. One-minute she was thinking she had lost her husband, and the next having a very slim chance for bringing him back. But at least if he were here a year or two, it would give him a chance to see Eirwen get married, and she would have her dad there with her on that special day. Zillah had no idea what to do. Her thoughts swayed from being selfish and having him nearby to wondering what kind of quality of life he would have if he were here longer. *If it's only for two years, it can't be that great, and he would most likely be suffering. Maybe it's not the best choice, and he just needs to rest.* She began thinking to herself.

Twenty-five minutes had passed when she realized she was still staring at the first page of the document, pondering all the scenarios that could happen if she picked one way or the other. Right on cue, she looked up and saw the general coming around the corner with his people following him again. *Do they ever take a break?* She released the tension in her shoulders in despair. She just needed a little more time. With that, in a self-desperation move and not ready to let Jorge go yet, she scrolled to the last page and clicked "accept." The device prompted her to scan her fingerprint and complete the acceptance sequence. Despairingly she accepted the terms and completed the arrangement.

As the general approached, she picked up the tablet and handed it back to him as he stopped in front of her.

"Just bring him back to us. We could use a little more time with him," Zillah pleaded with the general, as if he could change destiny.

"Ma'am, we will do what we can, but we can't make any promises. He is advanced farther than anyone we've done this procedure on. We don't know if this will bring him back, but we are willing to try. I will expedite the orders. You might want to visit him before we begin. If it doesn't go well, you may not see him again. I hope it works out. Good luck, ma'am," the general said and retreated down the hall from where he had arrived.

She walked the short distance to Jorge's room amidst the construction and hustle around the floor. After opening the door, she saw him covered and resting peacefully. The only movement was from the ventilator and oxygen tubes running to him. It appeared as though the doctors had attached some sort of blood filter machine to him. A nurse came in, and Zillah asked out of curiosity, "What is that machine? It wasn't there yesterday."

The nurse finished checking the saline units, turning toward Zillah, and replied,

"It's to oxygenate his blood. His lungs can't sufficiently distribute oxygen, so we had to add this machine. His organs will die if his blood isn't oxygenated," the nurse said.

Stunned at how fast he had gone downhill, Zillah held Jorge's hand.

"I'll give you a few minutes with him, but the military doctors will be taking him soon for the procedure," the nurse said.

"Thank you," was the only thing she could seem to get to come out of her mouth.

Shaken, exhausted, and still hungry, Zillah sat beside Jorge's bed. She wanted to cry, but somehow the emotion that frequently overcame her suddenly didn't want to visit anymore. Why, in her most desperate time, could she not shed a tear? As she held his hand, she began to whisper to him.

"Jorge, I don't know if you can hear me. I expect that it will register somewhere in there eventually, and you will remember. I love you! I'm doing this for you and for us. We need you here. I know you can pull through this. You've always been strong for us. They won't let me stay much longer, but always remember I love you."

She rested his hand beside his bed and covered it with the blankets that kept him warm. As she walked toward the door, several military doctors began to enter the room to adjust and transport Jorge. Zillah gave one look back, pressing her lips against her fingers, and blew him a kiss for luck and a temporary goodbye. A nurse intercepted Zillah on the way out of the room.

"Here is the general's contact information. It's not his direct line, but they can get you in touch with him. The government is transporting Jorge to a facility for the procedure, and we will update you when we have further information."

Zillah took the card and walked toward the elevator. The laborers had already painted the entryway since she first arrived. *What kind of operation is this?* It raised many red flags on Zillah's radar, but she was so consumed with Jorge's state that she ignored most of them and only pondered the surgery's outcome.

She continued to the ground level to depart the hospital. It was such a whirlwind of events. She didn't know if she could concentrate even if she went back to work. Although she didn't want to get into details, she called Garret.

"Hi, Garret, I'm kind of in shock right now," Zillah began.

"What's going on?" he replied.

"A general from the military came in and offered to do an experimental surgery on Jorge. I didn't know what to do," she said with a defeated voice.

"That's great. When will he be out?"

"It's just experimental, and he only has a fifteen percent chance of survival," she said.

"Wow," Garret replied.

"I'm going to go home and rest. I'm not sure my mind can handle much else today. It may be a few days before I return," she continued. Garret didn't say much other than conveying that his thoughts and prayers were with her, and they could keep things moving at work until she returned.

It was a long ride home from the hospital. Although Zillah often drove home alone after visiting Jorge, for some reason, this ride felt like the first ride when they returned from the hospital many years ago. She paused when getting out of the car. Instead of putting her headgear on, she stepped out of the vehicle and stood tall, as Jorge did that day. Feeling the sun through the spotted glass, caressing and warming her face. Feeling the heat of the sun at that moment made it feel like Jorge was standing beside her again. As her memories had been faded together, she remembered he wasn't actually there with her, then the moment disappeared.

She entered the house, which seemed to be foreign at this point. She just wanted to forget the day and have Jorge back with her, enjoying those laughing moments when they flirted and talked for hours. The intimate dinners and wine they occasionally shared. Sometimes that hadn't happened as often as either of them wanted, since they were focused on their work. It did seem to make those few moments even more memorable. A flood of memories filled her mind, so many years of good times with her loving husband. The hard times and arguments they had seemed to escape her memory and fall to the wayside. She began to pour a glass of wine as the tender moments flooded her mind again. The tears finally found their way back. They seemed to cool the pain of the situation, if only for a moment or two. The last tear chased the others to her chin as her glass was nearly full.

Picking her glass up that was now full of wine, she sipped the red concoction that temporarily numbed her mind. She removed her outer clothing and haphazardly threw it across the floor as she traveled through the house. Ordinarily, she was tidy and organized throughout her life. But something was broken, and she didn't have it in her to mind such trivial things. Climbing the steps, she crossed the house to the bedroom. Still hanging in the closet was the suit that Jorge had been wearing when they met Goramaius. She took a long drink of wine and reached down, clenching where the suit had been torn by the rocks that infected Jorge's leg. It seemed like a lifetime ago since they went on that trip. The remaining memories of the journey hung in the closet in front of her. She wondered how something so minuscule could take her Jorge away.

Music was playing in the background as Zillah continued to think about their history together. She couldn't help but wonder if he would still be around if they hadn't met and traveled to Missouri that day. But at the same time, maybe she wouldn't be where she was in her career either. They definitely wouldn't have a beautiful daughter that they raised together. And no possibility of grandchildren if he hadn't been around.

Most would say her feelings were bittersweet, as they tossed back and forth with such emotion: the good side and happy thoughts battling the sad and demonstrative thoughts. Throughout the night, she went back and forth on all the positive and negative things that the two had experienced. She filed the memories away in her mind, flushing her mental cache with more wine. Zillah even went through some of the things Eirwen left behind after she moved. So many memories and loving moments, even with them working long hours on the numerous Zander projects.

She continued drinking wine and mourning Jorge through the night until she couldn't continue anymore. She collapsed on the bed, temporarily numb to the world. A single beam of light shone through the window mid-morning the next day, illuminating flakes of dust settling in the room as the phone began to ring. Wincing from the wine the previous night and the headache that accompanied it, Zillah answered the phone.

"Hello," she said with a raspy voice.

"Hey Zillah, have you heard anything about Jorge yet? Someone in a military uniform came by looking for you a little while ago," Garret said with a concerned tone.

It took a moment for her to realize what was going on.

"I haven't... I don't... I'm not sure what is going on," Zillah said, barely hanging on to the phone. About that time, the chime sounded from the entrance door.

"Garret, I'll call you back; someone's at the door," Zillah said, somewhat groggy.

She grabbed a fluffy robe from the closet after stumbling out of bed. She looked down and shook her head as she saw the remains of the empty bottle of wine. She drank the last shot of wine in her glass, since her day was already starting off rough. A single ring stained the glass where the wine had sat for the last several hours.

A second ring on the doorbell sounded through the house as Zillah pulled her robe together and tied it off before taking the first step down toward the front door. She had a feeling she knew who was at the door, since not many people ever rang the bell or even visited. She opened the door. It was the general again, standing with his hat in hand as he usually did when addressing her. Two men accompanied the general this time instead of the four that had been at the hospital. It felt as though something was not quite right. The general spoke with his deep, authoritative voice and his typical well-pronounced words.

"Ma'am, I'm sorry to have to bring you this news. I thought it would be best to hear it from someone close to the situation and in person. Jorge passed early this morning from complications during the procedure. We brought you his effects. Due to the sensitive nature of the procedure, his body will be cremated. We will have a ceremony for him in a few days. Everything is taken care of. He died a hero."

Zillah broke down and continued to cry, even though she tried holding it together. He handed her a bag with items that were with Jorge that day. The general continued speaking as he gave her the bag.

"The state department would like to give tribute to him and memorialize him with honored veterans. They feel he served his duty to the cause and should receive a soldier's burial. I will send the details in the next few days. My condolences."

"I don't really have any words, General. Thank you for making the in-person visit to let me know," Zillah said with her voice shattering on each word.

The general turned toward a large, armored vehicle waiting in the compression bay near the road. Closing the door behind him, another rush of emotion filled her mind and body. She turned into a zombie as she sat at the table and stared out through the windows across the dry land. She was lost, and not even the wine would help at this point. Although there had been only a small chance of him making it though, she somehow held hope that he would make a recovery. She began to think to herself, *They wouldn't have suggested the procedure if it wasn't possible, right? Why would they give me false hope?* She pondered all kinds of thoughts that traveled through her mind the next couple of days, and one question led to another. Doubt, hurt, anger, and pain from losing her best friend of the last twenty years. Time had passed in a blur when she got the message about the funeral.

Zillah was getting dressed in her dark clothes to at least be presentable at the funeral. It was a military affair, after all. She walked across the bedroom to her closet, and the suit she was looking at days before stood out to her. Maybe it was something about Jorge's blood that had soaked the suit. Something about the way it was cut where his leg was injured. Grabbing a pair of scissors, she tried cutting the red section out of the leg area, but the material didn't budge. Snatching the suit off the hanger, she quickly went to the garage. She tried all sorts of tools but didn't have any luck. Not even the saws or shears would penetrate the material. She began to think again. *How could he have injured his leg, and the rock tore the fabric, if it is this strong? Was my suit the same?* She grabbed the same scissors and ran to the closet again. The scissors went right through the material. Her suit was just an ordinary suit, like so many others had worn. It only protected against the air elements. So many questions, but then an idea crossed her mind. She went back to the garage and found a hand-held plasma cutter that Jorge had in his toolbox.

The material from Jorge's exosuit began to glow. Finally, sparks flew, and the material separated where she had heated it. She extracted a square piece from the leg of the suit. If anything could draw her attention away from the fact that she just lost her husband, it was a good conspiracy.

She was confused about how they had different suits. Jorge's appeared highly impermeable, yet still, he got injured when he slipped. She briefly thought about the drug that Goramaius gave Jorge that day, then shrugged it off as too much of a coincidence if he was involved. She rolled the material separately and stuffed it in one of her pockets and hurried down the steps to the car that was waiting. It was early morning, and the sun hadn't risen yet, only a layer of dew that had formed on the windows.

The car ride was about thirty minutes to a building in the middle of nowhere. Funerals were different in this era. Nobody was buried anymore, only cremated. It seemed odd to Zillah that he would get a military funeral from merely being a contractor. But since it was a military send-off, officials coordinated the event in a large building with a wall of windows facing the East. As the morning sunrise pierced the night and the sun peaked over the horizon, the general concluded his words, and three volleys were fired. Following the shots, a cannon fired outside the building facing the sun. Ash plumed upward and dissipated as the sun showed through the cloud of smoke rising through the air. The general accepted the folded flag and brought it to Zillah for her keepsake.

"He was a fine man. He did this land a great service. His nobility and contribution will be remembered by all," the general said, concluding his speech. Zillah had lost her face of tears in the last several days. Doubt and anger were beginning to set in as she disbelieved what had actually happened.

Zillah walked to the wall opposite the windowpanes and looked at Jorge's memorial. Others migrated to a banquet room for brunch held in a nearby auditorium. The monument was a picture frame with a bust protruding in his likeness that was made of bronze. She still didn't understand why he had gotten such honor from the military. He hadn't served in any of the forces when he was younger. She would have known about it. This was something that highly honored generals got or, at the very least, someone that died valiantly in battle. It just didn't make sense.

She brushed her fingers across his name, reading the inscription. ***Jorge Ruthven 2276-2329 A distinguished gentleman who stood the test of time***. Well, he was a distinguished gentleman. Admittedly, Zillah also recognized that he was handsome and quite strong. She pulled the red-colored swatch from Jorge's suit out of her pocket and pinned it behind the memorial of her husband. It felt right to leave something of his that could stay with his memory. Straightening the frame, her finger paused at the edge just before letting go, and she walked to a table where everyone was congregated.

Conversations and stories flowed from the mouths of friends and family about the great things Jorge had done. He was kind and giving. Even in his angry streaks or when he unintentionally hurt people's feelings, he meant the best and didn't want harm for anyone. He strived to make people better for having known him, and maybe he would bring a little peace or joy to their lives. He wanted to change the world from the inside. Many people conversed about how he had helped them when they needed it or was a friend when nobody was around. He seemed to have a way that lit the room, even when nobody spoke with him and he felt invisible. You could feel the love and admiration in the people joining in the room from the stories they told. Distant tables burst into laughter as they listened to one tale after another. Above all, nobody could dispute that he had a love of Christ that he wanted to share with everyone.

As the day turned to afternoon, the crowd dissipated, and there were only a few souls left that had migrated to a table in the corner. Music was still playing lightly in the background as they began to wrap up their conversations. And with a few hugs, the last of the mourners paid their respects and went on about their evenings. It was a violently short few days, full of such emotion that not many could handle. Maybe it was for the best that she had transitioned into a new state of mind. She felt re-centered. Yet, for some reason, it wasn't as if she let go. She had simply moved her thoughts in a new direction. Deep down, she felt Jorge was still out there somewhere, waiting for her. Waiting for her to transition.

MOVING FORWARD

Nearly a year had passed since she lost Jorge. Zillah had several new interns, including Eirwen. Ravyn had been promoted and took some responsibility for Jorge's positions he previously mastered. She wasn't quite up to speed yet, but Ravyn made tremendous progress and had an excellent feel for what she was doing. Soon the team would be working with a new machine that was smooth and revolutionary to them. It wasn't like the drones they had sent to the past previously. Although it hadn't arrived yet from the drone division, it was up-to-date, new technology, and fast.

Zillah was sitting in her office behind her desk, working on mission plans. Since Jorge passed, she made Garret move to a different office, reinforcing her leadership role with the larger group. It just wasn't the same with Jorge gone. Since her division had grown the last year, she wanted to reinforce her leadership role with more division between herself and her subordinates. She began delegating more of her responsibilities to others, to have more time to plan how they would interact with the past. As she sat at her desk, she recovered the square piece of material that had been found in the Quarksandrium. She kept it hidden in the back of her desk drawer. It was only material, but something about it made her feel closer to Jorge. Almost like a common thread that wove their past together on the painful journey they had shared.

She began to wonder if it was really the material she liked having so close, or the fact that it was so similar to the piece she had cut from Jorge's suit. Maybe it was just a thought that linked the two cloth pieces that reminded her of him and touched her inner heart the way it had. When things got rough, she would reach for it, clenching it to absorb whatever mental strength she could gather, then returned it to her desk drawer—all the way in the back, behind paperwork and the office paraphernalia she had accumulated, waiting for the next time she needed a draw of strength. She was almost like the portal, drawing power from the Quarksandrium. As she closed her drawer, there was a loud knock on the door.

"Zillah, the new drones are here," Garret said excitedly from the other side.

"I'll meet you in the bay," she said through the door.

Shortly after Zillah arrived in the bay, the large skylight doors opened on the facility's roof where the Quarksandrium resided. The portal was on the northwest side, but the bay doors opened on the southeast side. A large transport craft was delivering three large crates to the Quarksandrium team in the bay area. They had been waiting for these to be completed for quite a while.

The transport vehicle was a substantial size and used several propulsion engines to hover while carrying a sizable payload. A Newsom 6-430 was a modern flying marvel. It was about the same size as a Chinook. But with the technology found in the last several hundred years, it was far more maneuverable and able to carry double its own weight in cargo. As the transport moved above the open bay doors, the first large crate began to descend into the arena. The containers were stacked with cables suspending the next box below it.

As it neared the ground, it hovered inches above the floor when the all-clear was given. A mechanical release was triggered, then dust and debris shot out from under the crate as it slammed to the floor. Dust rolled around the edges and sides of the box, hugging its bottom panels as it lay on the ground. The next two crates followed in the same manner, lined evenly across the open room. Soon after the last drone's box was released, a loud, high-pitched squeal emerged from the Newsom engines as it pitched upward, and it was gone.

Gears and motors began to pull the large bay doors closed over the sizeable portal's theater. The vacuum pumps' lingering sound continued the next half hour until the air had cycled within the large room. Soon warning lights changed from red to yellow. The system had to complete two refresh cycles to validate the air was clean and safe before members could move around without an exosuit. The lights would soon change from yellow to green, releasing the air-locked doors around the bay area.

This was like an early Christmas for the team. The interns could barely contain themselves at all the excitement. Zillah had given orders that they could unbox one of the drones and complete the setup list. They were to be ready for flight in three weeks. Two interns grabbed some tools and began removing the bolts that lined the large box's outer edge. They moved from one side to the next until all the security bolts were removed. The sides moved only slightly with the bolts removed. The massive box wasn't ready to reveal its contents yet, only teasing workers with what could be inside. They unwrapped a control box and pulled the long umbilical cable from under the skid of the crate. There were only two simple buttons on the control: close and open.

One of the workers stretched the cord out to one of the corners to get out of the way when the box expanded and used both thumbs to press the large OPEN button. A loud POP! came from the box as the pistons engaged and began to fill with fluid. The walls cracked open and started to reveal the contents long-awaited from the drone developers. As the sides opened like a flower, the light began to show the magnificent craft waiting inside: a sleek hybrid shape, somewhere between a circle and a triangle with rounded tips and edges. It was strange to see such an incredible craft that was thought to be an alien ship in historic times.

It was the second most commonly seen UFO in history. Rumors and conspiracies of aliens made it all the way to mainstream news media. Back then, they called it a UFO, an unidentified flying object. Ironically, today it was identified as a UFO drone, which meant Ultra-rapid Featherweight Organometallic drone. It was dark matte gray in color when turned off and didn't have any markings on it.

"Wow," one of the engineers marveled. Her awe-struck eyes glided across the large vehicle. It was smooth everywhere and a very sleek-looking machine. Zillah joined the crew in the hangar shortly after they opened the box.

"It is impressive. Isn't it?" Zillah admired.

"More than I ever imagined. Although, I do see an issue with this situation," Garret said in agreement.

"What's wrong with this situation?" Zillah asked.

"Well, from what I can tell, the portal is smaller than the drone," Garret's responded.

It was more than Zillah was ready to hear. "You have got to be kidding me. How did we not accommodate the new size? We just expanded the portal, right?" she began, raising her voice. After taking a breath to relax, she continued.

"It's not my fault. You said twenty yards. The drones

are close to twenty-five yards wide," Garret said with frustration.

"We'll just have to rotate the portal and leave it on the ground. It might work out better anyway, since we were planning on vertical escape routes on these new missions. Let's expand the portal and get the project moving," Zillah said with a sense of urgency.

"We've done it before. It shouldn't take as long this time," Garret commented.

Garret took the lead on the project to expand the portal. It took an additional three weeks to rotate and mount the portal to the floor. It ended up being far more extensive than Garret expected. Spanning a fifty-yard diameter, the portal was almost twice the size of the drone. Garret decided this was a great time to create a queue to the portal to allow for the next portal opening at a specific time and location. The queue parts and equipment would be ordered, but the software wouldn't be enabled for quite some time. The programming for that kind of task was intricate and needed many rolling features that allowed one slot to move to the next place in line. It wasn't optimal, but they could still use the traditional primary portal settings until it was complete.

The team toiled over the correct placement of the portal for the next few weeks. Sometimes Garret's words fell on deaf ears, but he always managed to bring the team back around to get his way and the project back on track. Younger generations seemed to have more ideas and malleable minds. Eventually, they tend to always end up with the same resolutions that the experienced team had already suggested. Usually, it was the experience that skipped the steps that wouldn't work to get the final thought in the process. It wasn't that they weren't valid or good ideas. They just took an awkward path that took longer to accomplish than the seasoned professionals had envisioned.

During the time the team spent building the portal, Zillah worked on the new queue code. It didn't seem like a big undertaking, but it would prove mischievous in the future. It's incredible how being tired and grieving can push a person to overlook the most delicate details.

As the portal was approaching completion, Zillah decided to prepare the ship and put aside programming for a while. She went to the ship's hull and marveled at its beauty. The dark-skinned craft had a cloaking image membrane integrated into its surface. Pinhead-sized cameras covered the external body, giving views from all angles. They were used to project images from the opposite side of the craft on the membrane. The ship was built for speed and agility, but cloaking was currently impossible at high speeds. Usually, when cloaking was activated during movement, the drone would just appear as a lighted object. The drone designers still had many bugs to work out with the cloaking technology. Yet they let the project proceed anyway, since it wouldn't hurt the maneuverability of the drone.

She ran her hand on the outer skin of the UFO, feeling the tiny bumps and ridges around the ship, taking in the design and location of the small cameras and sonic modifiers. The ultrasonic modifiers were necessary to smooth and counterbalance air displacement when the craft accelerated rapidly, removing shock waves and air turbulence. It offered a nearly invisible signature to 21st-century radars. Her hand moved under its belly, and she pressed upward in the center with the medallion in one hand. The circular hatch released and began to extend, protruding to reveal a perfect insertion place for the sizeable coin-shaped relic. As she pressed firmly, the object snapped into place, and the hatch began to slowly retract back into a locked position. She took a step back and watched the craft give off a brief sequence of lights across the membrane of the vessel. It went through a series of diagnostic checks, verifying that all the functions interacted correctly. Even the marriage sequence of the relic with the UFO was quite spectacular to view.

After closely examining the craft, Zillah gathered the rest of the team. Her team had expanded to eight people in all: five in the control room and three in the event room where the Quarksandrium equipment was housed. Her daughter Eirwen managed the drone field and the event room, even though she was finishing her internship. Eirwen also recently got married. He was working an alternate station in the back of the control room. It somehow seemed strange how a close family seemed to be running and operating a government-funded time travel operation.

"OK, everyone, we have the first drone configured. We need to run the list before we can jump. Let's get on our stations and make sure we get this right before we make the first run," Zillah called out to the team as they huddled in a circle.

As they dispersed, the group split into two, heading to their respective stations. One station in the bay monitored the drone and a variety of settings. A second station monitored the portal and redundant settings for stability. The third was a pivot station. It watched the interaction between the other two stations and was where Eirwen managed her team.

In the control center, Zillah commanded the UFOd while two others watched from mirrored stations. They would be piloting the additional drones in future missions. Besides Garret, Ravyn was closest to Zillah's expertise. She was brilliant and learned very quickly how to manipulate the group without them feeling she was bossy.

They all prepared as the drone cycled its lights, sitting on the control pad, waiting for its next command. Zillah called out for launch cycles to begin as the portal powered up. Only half power was needed to control the drone, but they would need full power to stabilize the doorway to the past and tear time. It was still only a brief three-minute window, but that was plenty of time to move the drone thought. As the units were powered up and the Quarksandrium approached fifty percent power, the drone switched from cycling standby lights to full system integration with all the control room systems.

"OK, hold fifty percent, and we'll test the drone," Zillah commanded as she began running sensor tests on the drone. She tested the cameras, switching from various vantage points of the drone. She noted the heat signatures and warm spots of the portal with the infrared cameras. The various colors of red, blue, green, and yellow contrasted images were spectacular on her displays.

"Lights out."

Zillah called out on the communication devices. Shortly after the lights went out, she tested night vision. This would definitely be advantageous for night missions. Although the green hue wasn't as vivid as the infrared, it accomplished its task. It reminded her of a deeper rich-colored dusk in their current environment.

"Lights on, please."

She called after she returned the optics to the standard-setting. She began zooming in on various objects across the room, moving around the room to see all the different angles, transitioning between cameras. So far, everything appeared to be functioning correctly. She went through systems tied to the cameras. She used the workers in the bay to test facial recognition, remote biometrics, and object identification. She then switched to object density and object obscured imaging modes that could see through some items, even at a distance.

"Flightpath check."

She called to the control room. Soon after, the drone lifted off its base of the box and hovered quietly above the ground. Zillah manipulated the console, switching virtual buttons on the screen, making gestures with her hands, and typing on a flat virtual keyboard projected on the table. She wore bands across her fingers that detected motion, taps, and gestures that helped her fly the futuristic craft.

Suddenly, a bright light appeared around the ship, and it darted across the length of the bay. Within seconds it went hundreds of yards. It was something no human-crewed aircraft could do because of the g-forces produced in such a maneuver. Zillah continued waving her hands, making changes to settings, and telling the craft how to react.

As with any computer system, there were several modes. The interactive mode would allow the pilot to fly in a traditional sense, allowing them to control it in real time. An additional configuration mode would enable her to program the drone's movements ahead of time and then execute the actions. She completed the flight path test with gestures, keystrokes, and settings on the screen, finishing it with a simple gesture that would execute. She brought her hands close to her chest with opposite palms facing each other, like she would have been embracing a ball. Zillah twisted and spun her wrists, rotating the invisible ball in her hands. Then with a quick movement, her hands clenched, ripping the nonexistent ball apart. At that moment, the drone made several erratic moves, darting back and forth, zigzagging back toward the control room.

The drone flew across the long room within seconds. When it came time to test the cloaking, Zillah didn't say a word before changing the settings. Suddenly cloaking took over in the last few feet of its travel. It emitted a bright light, then swiftly disappeared when it stopped, as everyone in the bay gasped. It stopped inches from the glass that divided the control room from the holding bay.

"Where did it go?" one of the bay attendants asked.

Zillah couldn't help but give a smirk as she morphed the drone back to being visible. Amazingly, it had returned as quickly as it had retreated to the distant side, even with the sharp corners. It was almost incomprehensible how fast it could move, pivoting on the tiniest scale. With the test complete, Zillah briefly went over the flight plan. The drone still hovered in the bay while they looked through the historical logs of their next mission. The exact timing and moments they would need to execute their flight path were critical. Yet, it had already happened, so they knew the precise timing that would be required of them.

CLOSE ENCOUNTER

"Full power," Zillah commanded as Garret had a sheepish grin on his face.

"You got it," Garret returned sharply.

The center orb of the Quarksandrium began to glow and gyrate on the floor. Sparks began to fly as power increased to capacity. A translucent wave of energy flowed from the center to the portal's outer edges, engulfing everything between. As the power continued to grow, reaching maximum capacity, the device's center pulsed and rippled toward the outer edge as a black abyss overtook the portal.

"It's stable," Garret called out.

Their first mission back through time with the new configuration was underway. The UFOd hovered over the portal, and suddenly, as Zillah spread her arms apart, the craft dropped through the portal as if it were free-falling. It looked as though it fell into a pond of water, only there was no splash. The abyss' ripples continued even after the craft had left until it gradually settled and went back to a sort of calm dark water.

After a few minutes had passed and the portal normalized, Garret made the call to reduce power as he moved the virtual dials.

"Return to operation power."

The portal closed, and only the orb remained lit with its lights and gyrations.

"We're good. I still have connection and visuals," Zillah said as she maneuvered the craft. She waved her hands and arms around instinctually while watching the cameras on her screens. It was almost like an old first-person virtual reality game she was playing, except this was actually happening. It was the first view they'd seen live in the past. It was incredible. The sky was clear, and the visual they saw was nothing like they expected. Many of the crew had never seen clear blue skies.

It was July in the year 1969. Zillah hovered the craft twenty-five miles above Earth's surface. She held the position with the UFOd for a while, watching the ground from a distance. A few clouds were passing near the terrain and ocean underneath. At that moment, a pinhead-sized white cloud appeared below and began to grow like a worm.

"There it is," Zillah said as she tilted her head slightly to the side, then forward.

She knew it would happen but was still enamored with how technology had been created and evolved over the years. The cloaking on the ship was turned on, so the UFO appeared invisible even if someone had a telescope. Zillah adjusted the ship's cloaking to include only the bottom half of the vessel. She intended this mission to be like a beacon to warn those in the past. She needed to covertly let them know what was in their future.

As the cloud structure grew, so did the object that created it. The Saturn V left an unmistakable trail of smoke and vapor behind. As the ship got closer, she wiggled with anticipation, trying to get situated in her seat for an exciting ride. Her objective was to lead the rocket enough that it wouldn't interfere with their mission yet would give them a visual warning of what was to come. The rocket was approaching quickly, and when it was several hundred feet away, she jerked her hands to one side, engaging the hyper-drives on the drone. The drone promptly maintained speed and was alongside the rocket for at least thirty miles before one of the rocket's stages separated. She saw the three occupants of the *Apollo* for quite some time, but she wasn't sure if they saw the drone. As the first stage separated, she maneuvered the UFOd back to where it began.

"Wow, that was intense," she commented as she took a deep breath and tried to calm down from the adventure.

"OK, let's park this thing and get ready for the next mission," Zillah said.

She sped farther out in the ocean before diving and splashing down, driving the ship to the depths of the ocean. A while later, the drone's radar indicated that the craft was nearing the ocean floor, and she lightly set the drone on the bottom and powered it down.

"Impact, power the Quarksandrium down," she said, indicating that the drone had touched down at its destination.

"Powering down," Garret said, repeating the order back for verification. With that, he began turning switches off in sequence. The device began losing the intensity of light as the whirring sounds of spinning devices began to slow to a stop.

"OK, everyone, great mission. Let's finish our paperwork and meet in the conference room in two hours for a debrief," Zillah announced over the intercom while she gathered her items and headed for her office.

As she returned to her office, she made notes in her mind, which she would later document for the team. She wanted to replay the footage from the rocket's interaction to see if there was any indication that the astronauts saw the drone. She played and replayed the encounter several times forward, backward, and in slow motion. There was nothing to indicate that they saw them. However, it was difficult to tell since the movement in their suits was limited. They could have turned their heads without the helmet moving much, in those days. The shadows and glare from the rocket were just enough to prevent the drone's cameras from capturing a detailed image of its passengers. Even the different camera recordings of various modes were obscured. The speed and material of the orbital must have blocked the drone's cameras.

It was an intense and quick ride. Most likely, the astronauts would have been focused on their instruments instead of looking out the window. Time would tell, but there was always a chance they wouldn't confide in anyone even if they did see something. It could have been passed off as an illusion or launch anomaly that was just convincing their brains they saw something. There could have been a thousand and one reasons to explain away what they thought was impossible, as just a figment of their imagination.

Zillah closed the program and finished her notes. She included the craft's location, distances of closest ships, land, and others that could have spotted the UFOd. The team needed this information to scan newspapers and other potential UFO-sighting distributions. Even with cloaking engaged while maintaining the high speed alongside the rocket, it may have made the drone look like a white orb or ghost reflection from the rocket's flare. She quickly saved all the points of interest in the mission and headed to the conference room to meet the team. It was essential to document interactions or potential sightings, because even the smallest encounter in the past could make a change in the future.

She walked through the mission they had just completed with her group without leaving any detail to speculation. All the potential sightings were divided among the group. Even with the bay workers researching events after a mission, it was a long, tedious process. Having the whole team research would make the next mission come around sooner. Although it didn't really matter how long it took, they would still be able to go to a specific point in time and reactivate the drone for the next mission.

Everyone exited the conference room and headed to their office area, only later to meander around the archive room, searching for relevant articles. Sometimes they found traces of where they had been through articles in random conspiracy papers and website archives, depending on what period in time they were researching. It usually took a couple weeks to review events. Although a few weeks sounds like a long time, it took three people several months to scour through an overnight mission, in the beginning. They always made sure nothing had significantly changed from each incident.

The team's first mission was complete with the new drone, and the next mission was fast approaching. It was nice to expand the possibilities with a quicker, more recent, and more versatile ship. Zillah was in her office deciding on plans for the next mission. With the speed and agility of the new drone, the options were nearly limitless. She could pick any event in the following years. Her instructions from the board were her only guidelines, and even those were vague—primarily, avoid contact to prevent changes in the future, and document the events. Since this was only their second mission with the new craft, she decided to follow orders and pick something reasonably simple to investigate.

When Zillah finally decided on an event, it was still relatively large. The drone had been sitting on the ocean floor for seventeen years. If the UFOd was made of material from centuries past, it would have eroded and been lost forever. The newer technology and newly created metal compounds from the Quenomoly allowed it to withstand the corrosion from an abusive ocean.

They set the portal's jump time for October in the last five minutes of Halloween, just before the hour of a new day, 1985. They went through the typical sequence of powering all the equipment and instruments as they usually would. The orb was powered to half intensity to connect with the drone. Zillah began to take over the drone that was sitting at the bottom of the ocean. She moved through the power sequence and verification of all the instruments and functions.

"OK, everything looks good. Let's begin heading north," Zillah said with enthusiasm. She waved her hands, and the craft jumped off the ocean's floor. Several of the other monitors had several camera views from the drone. There wasn't much to see in standard view, since it was so dark at that depth, except for the occasional glowing fish or debris that would float by the drone. Zillah decided to change the images to thermal and sonar. They also used a refractive light technology that emitted an invisible beam. From there, the sensors could develop areas where it dissipated or refracted against objects. It was like sonar, but since light travels faster, it had a faster response. Although LiDAR had been around for hundreds of years, enhancements had been made that gave spectacular details, especially underwater.

As the UFO went north underwater, it went faster than any other craft could go. Yet, it would still take several hours to get to their destination. Since vehicles were scarce underwater, it was easier for them to go unnoticed. They would make their presence known when they wanted to, but not until then. Interactions needed to be planned ahead of time and methodically. Some instances might be inevitable, but overall, they would be coordinated and more frequent as the time approached the Quenomoly.

Nearing the destination just before two in the morning, it was another epic time in history. The LiDAR picked up a large object ahead of the craft.

"This must be it," Zillah said to the group as a sunken ship's hull came into view. She angled the drone to make contact with the abyssal plain, churning up sediment in the process to cover most of the drone. With the sensors and cameras, they could still see what was happening. In a matter of minutes, a smaller vehicle whirred in front of them that was tethered to

the surface. As the motors stopped on the submersible, the UFO picked up vibrations traveling through
its tether from the surface. It was the crew of the ship
cheering briefly before realizing what morbid anniversary they were celebrating. The *Titanic* was a majestic and the most extensive cruise ship of its time. The
drone team's original plan was to dart quickly in front
of the camera with lights flashing in a patterned sequence, but something wasn't quite right.

She tried to regain control of the UFOd after witnessing the preceding events of the underwater mu-
seum. Zillah moved her hands to gradually bring the
drone out of the sludge and debris on the bottom of
the ocean, but nothing happened.

"What is going on? Everything looks normal on the
instruments," Zillah asked as she scanned the drone's
instrument displayed in her glasses. The flight glasses
were a heads-up display, allowing her to see important
flight information, similar to a fighter pilot in years past.
She clicked through some of the screens with her eye-
lids. Her eyes were the mouse on the computer in this
case. Different informational screens popped up, and
she expanded them to her monitors on the desk. As
she combed the diagnostic data, nothing appeared to
be wrong. All the systems were reading normal. As she
scanned the instruments, she saw a flicker in some
of the readings; then she lost her connection with the
UFOd. It went dark—all the ship's information was
lost. She waved her arms and clicked through screens.

QUARKSANDRIUM: THE BEGINNING

Nothing happened. It was as if it just disappeared.

"Power it down! We need to figure out what happened, and quick!" Zillah yelled frantically.

"I didn't see anything until you lost connection, then the load readings on the Quarksandrium vanished. It seemed like a motor running without the car around it. There was no resistance," Garret replied on the open communication channel.

"That's what I saw down here too," Eirwen said, corroborating his story.

"OK, get all the documentation, settings, and all the information you have on this mission prepared, and we'll meet in the conference room," Zillah said abruptly.

She shook her head, tossed her glasses on the desk, and aggressively slid the chair under the desk in disgust. Zillah walked out of the room, trying to figure out what had just happened. She mentally sifted through every moment of the mission. Minutes of the mission quickly passed her memory as she walked through the door to her office. Opening her email, she found a request from the board for a meeting.

"Well, isn't this just great," she muttered to herself.

They seemed to find the worst times to call meetings. Luckily it wasn't till next week, and they could run one more mission before then. Maybe she could put things in a better light if she could get the drone back. Through the next few hours, she gathered information about what happened at the *Titanic* site. Perhaps it was cursed. After all, it had already taken down one mighty ship. She collected the information she needed for the meeting and went to the conference room. Generally, it was a tablet, laptop, and all the related electronic data she had gathered.

Shortly after lunch, they began arriving for the debrief in the conference room.

"OK, it looks like we have most everyone here. Where's Eirwen?" Zillah asked.

"She was reviewing the logs in the bay the last time I saw her," one of the members answered.

"Well, let's give her a few more minutes, and we'll begin. Everyone needs to be here for this to make sure we cover all the angles," Zillah said. About then, Eirwen squeezed through the door and slid into her chair near one end of the table.

"Has anyone found any anomalies with the drone that we weren't expecting? We also need to find out why it wasn't functioning and why we lost contact with it," Zillah began.

"I am pretty sure I have found the reason why we lost contact with the drone, but I'll save that for after we figure out what happened to it," Garret said with a knowing attitude.

"That's why I was late. I think I may have found out what went wrong, or at least from what I can tell. It looks like there may have been a leak in one of the areas of the drone. I can't tell exactly why, though. Maybe it was weakened when it hit the ocean floor.

There were false readings up until a few seconds before we got disconnected. The energy core is nearly drained, but we might have enough to get it back close to us. I don't know what other systems are affected, but we need to find a way to get that dried out quickly," Eirwen asserted.

"What about the Halon systems? If we activate those, do you think it would be enough to force the water out long enough to get it airborne?" Gryffen, Eirwen's husband, began with a sudden idea.

"That might work," Zillah replied with a little excitement.

"Let's look for a place that can hide the drone a couple hundred years, and we'll move on to the next mission," Zillah said to the crew. They all looked through their tablets and laptops at nearby places that the drone could be stored.

"What about some of the caves to the south?" One of the team asked.

"I'm not sure we can navigate to the cave entrance and get deep enough to prevent anyone from finding the drone. Considering the lack of core energy remaining, it seems unlikely," Eirwen replied despairingly.

"What about the deep end of the Pecos River?" another team member asked.

"That actually may work. Let's look into that. We could wedge it in the deepest area. It looks to be about a thousand feet," Garret said, then continued with his analysis.

"OK, now that we know what happened and where we can put it, I believe we got disconnected from the drone because our next mission interrupted the signal from us."

Shocked faces began to look at him as he continued speaking after a brief pause.

"Zillah, you will have to do some extra coding, but we can break the signal and overtake controls in the next mission, so we don't lose time on the energy core," Garret concluded.

"Yes, that's it! It was us who interrupted the transmission. OK, let's prepare for the next mission. We'll begin the mission tomorrow morning. Let's go, people," Zillah proclaimed with excitement.

The next morning the team began showing up earlier than usual. The tension was a little higher than average, knowing that the group could lose the primary ship. Even worse, there was the possibility their technology could be discovered by a previous generation. Especially since a ship was already looking in the area around where the *Titanic* had sunk. Zillah had been working through most of the evening and into the morning programming the break in transmission. She was tired but ready to retrieve the craft.

The group was highly devoted; most came in early to clean or verify the equipment's settings before every mission. Zillah usually ran close to being on time wherever she went, sometimes a few minutes before, sometimes a few after, but always in a five-minute window. Even when she was exhausted, she was very dependable.

"Good morning, everyone," Zillah said over the communicators as she attached the device to her shirt. One by one, everyone replied with their version of a greeting for the new day. She could usually tell what kind of mood the crew was in by how the greetings went over the channels on launch day.

Zillah set the portal's clock to a few seconds before losing their connection to the UFOd. The program she wrote the day before would take a short time to interject and cut the previous connection they had to the drone in the past.

"OK, we're set. Half power, please," Zillah said across the communication devices, alerting everyone to bring the Quarksandrium online and go through the normal cycle of events preparing and getting the large beast to life. Their communication devices consisted of a tiny earbud and a buttoned microphone they could wear. The screens came online and began showing all the instruments as the green lights lit up like a starry city on a hillside from the control room. Zillah put her headgear and gesture rings on, preparing for the next part of the journey to interact with the scuttled saucer.

The program took control as it severed the previous linking their past selves had to the ship. It required a little extra power to the Quarksandrium, but it finally stabilized after interrupting the previous connection. As the link completed the synchronization, Zillah began to see instruments across her heads-up display. She clicked through a few menus with her eyes and saw what Eirwen was talking about with the low-power situation. She began clicking in the menus, deeper and deeper until she got to fire suppression. She changed the disbursal rate of the halon to forty percent, then activated the suppression systems. The drone's moisture sensors began to show the levels were decreasing, and suddenly she had control of the ship again. The mobile submersible was still in the area preoccupied with the *Titanic* wreckages. She began to steer away from them, heading south until she could exit the ocean unnoticed and soar to the skies.

The drone broke the surface of the water, leaving a long trail of salty water behind it. Continuing to drip slowly as the last of the water drained from the craft, Zillah darted above the clouds as quickly as she could. She also left a stream of cloud particulates and condensation behind the vessel as it burst through into a higher atmosphere. It was still dark in the early- morning hours, but as fast as the craft traveled, it would arrive at the Pecos River just after dusk. Hopefully, it would be dark enough that nobody would notice the strange saucer plunging into the water.

The dark drone shot across the open skies. Within fifteen minutes, it had traveled nearly four thousand miles. The energy core was almost depleted with the high strain to maintain speed. She maneuvered her hands as the drone began to fly below the clouds again. The distant river appeared on the horizon as the crew started to take sighs of relief. Unfortunately, there were a few boats at one end of the river. They soon realized they could enter around the bend without anyone seeing, since most boaters had ported for the evening.

Zillah navigated the ship downstream under the water to its resting place just short of one thousand feet below the surface. It was quite a ride, but the UFOd would sit until they retrieved it in the future. Zillah exhausted a sigh of relief and once again called the team to power down the drone and the portal, and complete their debrief process. Zillah bowed her head for a moment, giving thanks, along with releasing her muscle tension before she removed her gear.

"Thanks, everyone, great mission," she commented as she walked back to her office. She picked up the phone before even sitting down and immediately called the drone team. Harold picked up the other end of the phone. He was recently promoted to the lead after the success of the recent drone.

"Hey, Harold, I need some help recovering one of our crafts," Zillah began.

"What happened to it? Where is it at?" Harold asked.

"We had to stash it in a deep area of the Pecos River. It might be a bit heavy; it appeared to have a leak. How soon can we retrieve it?"

"I can scramble a team tomorrow morning. Would

that work?" Harold replied after looking at the calendar.

"Perfect. I will send you the coordinates and meet you there first thing."

The next day Zillah met the recovery team near where they maneuvered the ship deep in the crevasse. The same transport ship that delivered the vehicles to the Parlin Center landed a good-sized boat above where the drone was sitting in the water below. The team disconnected the vessel and began to use submersibles to connect the UFOd to the hovering transport ship above. It was a long process that took several hours to haul the underwater drone to the surface. Zillah and Harold were on the shore, overseeing the recovery process.

The Newsom heaved the heavy craft upward until the hull peaked through the water's surface. The nylon straps and netting cradled the ship allowing the water to drain and run freely out of the drone. Water continued dripping as the vessel dangled over the shoreline. Harold attached a magnetic power source to the drone as Zillah reached for the ship's center belly. The hatch reluctantly released as water drained out, and the door finally opened. She retrieved the medallion relic she had installed for the navigation of the UFOd.

"Thank you, Harold, for getting this done so quickly. I have to meet with the board next week, and at least I'll have some answers for them," Zillah said, reaching out her hand to shake Harold's.

"Not a problem. I'll let you know what I find when

we get it back to the lab. I'll also have your next drone ready to bring over in the next day or two," he delightfully informed her.

After returning to her office, she marveled at the relic she recovered from the drone. It hadn't aged or changed at all. She placed it on the red cloth in the back of her desk drawer and locked the drawer before leaving her office. With leaving critical information and physical items in her office, she had also removed access to anyone but herself. She requested the security team install multiple biometric devices to gain access to the room. It was a bit troublesome at times returning to her office, but at least she knew it was secure and nobody could get in.

DÉJÀ VU

The next drone was delayed a few days and arrived the morning Zillah was scheduled to meet with the board. The board members' dynamic had changed so much over the years, she wondered if it would be different this time too. A knock on the door interrupted her train of thought about the upcoming meeting.

"Dr. Ruthven, a drone is being delivered!" one of the team members shouted from behind the door.

"Thank you. Have Harold meet me in the control room," she said in acknowledgment. She briefly revisited her thoughts about the upcoming meeting with the board. Unable to concentrate, she gathered herself before locking up and heading across the hall.

"Morning, Zillah," Harold greeted her as she entered the room. Zillah couldn't help but look out the window at the bay at the large boxes being delivered.

"Morning, Harold. Looks like you've changed the delivery boxes," she said, recognizing that the boxes had a different texture and locking mechanism than the previous ones.

"Yes, after your last effort to destroy our work, we've upgraded the drones and the boxes. The new boxes have refueling and recharging capabilities. They will open mechanically without removing security bolts, and they can open and close on dry land or underwater. We've placed systems inside to extract the water from the box once the drone has returned to base. Also, the drone is capable of maneuvering with the box. It loses some speed, but it's still impressive. We also brought two extra boxes for the current drones you have. Over time, this should make them more reliable than the older ones," Harold enthusiastically explained, as if he were giving a sales pitch.

"That's great! I'll keep you updated on how they fare through the next sequence," she replied with acceptance.

When the delivery was complete, the team went back to their reports, continuing their research of the last mission they ran. The previous mission series was a little different, since they had to investigate significantly more years for activities.

Zillah had returned to her desk to finish preparing for the meeting with the board. She thought briefly about the meeting's different possible outcomes, then reached into the back of the center drawer. The medallion was resting on the square red cloth she had found in the portal. Staring endlessly through the relic, she flipped it over to study the engravings, then slid it into her pocket. Maybe it would bring her luck.

She clenched the red piece of cut cloth and thought of Jorge for a few moments before returning it to the back of the drawer and locking it. For Zillah, it wasn't the face value of the treasure she guarded in the drawer that mattered but the value to her heart, mental state, and hope for the future that meant the most. She left her office to go to the meeting as her office door locked behind her.

Zillah walked down the corridors and tunnels connecting the two buildings through the center of the Zander complex. She wondered what this meeting could be about as she walked and looked out the long line of windows that let sunlight into the tunnels between sites. As she approached the conference room doors, they split and magically opened as if someone were watching for her or knew the exact moment she stepped in front of the doors. When she walked through the door, she realized her suspicions were correct. The power had shifted again. Esther was no longer leading the meeting, at least not that she could tell. It was one of the beings in the crimson suits. This leader's cloak was also burgundy and had gold trim, while the other one to his left had black accents. There was also an empty seat to his right. It was a little strange that one of the chairs was open. The other four members were wearing green suits and green robes.

When the leader finally spoke, it sounded like his voice was being modulated. It was easily understood, but it didn't seem like his original voice.

QUARKSANDRIUM: THE BEGINNING

"What is your status on the project? I have heard you had issues on the last deployment," the leader began questioning.

"Yes, we had a few issues in the last mission series. A drone leaked after a rough landing in the ocean on the second leg of the mission. We resolved the problem using some unique procedures with the onboard systems. Subsequently, we moved it to a freshwater source that wouldn't further damage the vessel but kept it hidden till we could recover it. The drone squad upgraded the storage boxes and the leak issues with the drone to prevent it from happening again," Zillah explained to the leader.

"Where do you stand with your primary objective, the Quenomoly? And the secondary objectives that led to the events of the Quenomoly?" the leader inquired.

Zillah paused a minute to gather her thoughts and how she would answer. She knew this group was sometimes not a patient one. They always wanted things faster than she anticipated them moving.

"We haven't found the contamination source from the Quenomoly or any way to prevent it at this time. We will get there. As you know, many events are chained together through history. We have only begun to scratch the surface in this journey," she continued in an exhausted voice.

"I understand. Continue your quest. We must continue... our past depends on your future. Good luck," the leader said boldly.

The leader's voice seemed understanding but agitated as he gestured, outstretching his hand toward the door. As the door opened for her to exit, she couldn't help but remember when Goramaius said something similar. *What did he mean?* She racked her brain to what it could have meant as she retraced her steps back to her office. She began to notice the sunlight through the breezeway between buildings. It seemed different than when she passed through earlier, heading in the opposite direction. *Funny how lights and shadows reflected slightly differently can give such a different mindset and train of thought. Time is a construct that can change the path of anything in any direction.* She began wondering why they had called this meeting, if they already knew the issues with the drone and her progress. *Was it just to make me try to move faster? What is really going on here?* Sometimes this place was just weird, and she didn't understand how it all fit together, but she needed them as much as they needed her. She truly wanted to make a change that would be better for everyone.

She was nearly back to her office when she turned the corner and began walking down a long hallway. The hall continued several hundred feet beyond her door. She hadn't really been looking down the hall, only a few steps in front of her as her mind bounced from thought to thought. Her concentration was on post-meeting analysis and deciphering what was and wasn't said. When she arrived at the door, she finally looked up to enter the codes and input her biometrics.

Her eyes shifted and strayed down the long hallway as she caught a glimpse of flowing red material escape around the corner. Suddenly her heart raced, and goosebumps ran up her arms and the back of her neck. *What.* She began running down the hall as fast as she could. By the time she got to the end to look down the next hallway, whatever it was, was gone. Her heart was still racing as she tried to catch her breath from the long run. She didn't wait long before quickly walking back to her office. When she finished scanning her eye and handprint, the door opened, and she approached her desk, only pausing a moment before stepping around to the backside.

As she sat down behind the large desk, she pulled gently on the drawer. Thankfully, it was still locked. She took a deep breath and paused in relief. Maybe she just imagined the figure in the hallway. She was pretty tired, after all. She unlocked the drawer by placing her fingerprint under one of the corners of the drawer. It beeped and clicked as it unlocked and protruded slightly. Zillah reached all the way to the back of the drawer to recover the red swatch she had found in the Quarksandrium. Something was covering it. She froze in fear because it wasn't as she had left it. Zillah slid the drawer to its maximum extension, wondering what could possibly be in her drawer that wasn't there before.

Two more coin relics were resting on the red cloth.

A wave of chills suddenly covered her body again. This time they shot up one leg, both her arms and around one side of her face. Still frozen, looking at the back of the drawer, she glanced at her arms that still held her hair at a distance from her skin. That must have been the red cloak she saw down the hall, and it wasn't just her imagination. They looked very similar, the same size, but the marking on each medallion was different. They were in the same unreadable language, just like the original relic. She couldn't help but now wonder, *How many more coins could there be?*

She gathered her thoughts and the coins before she went to the bay to install the relics in the drones. She radioed Garret to meet her there with the rest of the crew. As she called them all together, she explained there were more relics for each of the drones, and they could run all three ships together. The additional people in the control room would take on more duties flying drones. Eventually, they would require more recruits to accommodate further missions. Still, they didn't have time to rest, the need to expand their search and keep progressing with their assignments to find answers was essential.

"We'll install the relics and run tests on the drones. They need to be resealed in the boxes and deposited in history. We will cover all the new procedures before launch," Zillah said.

As the workers scattered back to their stations in preparation for the next missions, Zillah found the button that released the crate's walls holding the drone captive. After the relics had synced with the UFOd's and other equipment, the containers could be opened remotely. Until then, they had to be opened manually. The box opened, flowering out until it reached the ground. As the sides opened, a new drone was revealed that looked identical to the other two, except it had a little bit more of a blue tint instead of just dark gray. Its surface was completely smooth, the hull was solid. Its sensors and cameras were moved inside the drone. The only opening she found was around where she inserted the relic. Zillah went through the process of installing all the relics in the saucers. After each hatch closed, the bay area began glowing with lights that cycled from one end to the other on the three drones. It seemed like a Christmas light show just for them.

All of the crew were at their stations reviewing charts and procedural information. Gryffen would be one of the pilots, along with one of the other interns, Alejandra, who had been shadowing Zillah. Zillah went through the checklist with the crew and brought the portal up halfway. After running through the new drones' testing, they returned them to their new cubes and shut down the devices. It would take several more test sessions before the new pilots would be ready to go on a mission, but there was other work to be done. Zillah concluded the test flights by sending thanks to the crew over the communication links and reminding them of the upcoming group meeting the following day.

Heavy-hearted, Zillah went back to her office. She felt something tugging at her but wasn't sure what it was. Something just didn't feel right about the situation, how the extra coins had appeared, and the board's overall push to get this done so quickly. Why had it escalated so quickly? She sat at her desk with her face in her hands, wondering how they had got this far. Was she really chasing her dream of restoring humanity, or was she just a pawn in some bigger game she wasn't aware of?

As she looked up, she instinctually logged into her computer and opened her calendar and tasks. There it was. How could she have forgotten? She had been focused on the next step instead of the big picture. With new ships being created and now flyable, they needed to complete the queue system for the crafts to arrive at the same time. They would eventually need to have looping designed to return to the hangar instead of storing the ships in the past. These were mostly programming issues, but they all needed to be addressed before their next mission.

She called Eirwen, Ravyn, and Garret into her office to plan how they would create the queue. As they all began to gather, she began explaining.

"I know we've spoken some about this before, but before we can go on any more missions, we need to address the queue issue," Zillah explained.

"What queue issues?" Ravyn questioned.

"The queue issue is, there is no queue," Garret retorted while rolling his eyes and shaking his head.

"Correct, Garret. We need to finish the queue system to send three ships that arrive simultaneously in the past. It's critical that even if our technology is seen, they won't equate it to being human-made machines. So, we need a queue system that allows one drone to go back in time. It will cycle to the next queue, and the second drone goes to the exact same time in an adjacent location," Zillah explained with a lack of technical detail.

"That makes sense," Ravyn said, nodding her head.

"Let's go ahead and build the queue to ten places. We don't have to enter all the slots for each mission. Still, it will allow us to expand and enter the return coordinates before the mission rather than during the mission. Also, the queue needs to be a separate module to the Quarksandrium. We already have all the equipment. It just needs to be built," Zillah continued explaining.

"What is our timeframe for completing this?" Eirwen asked as if she didn't already know the answer was going to be "yesterday."

"I am getting a lot of pressure from the board. They seem to know more than I do at times. They gave us two weeks to complete this, so let's get started immediately," she said.

As they separated and returned to their desks, they

collaborated about who would take what parts of the task.

"I believe Zillah has a large set of programming completed for the queue," Garret said to Ravyn as they walked to the control room.

At the same time, Eirwen finished constructing the physical components of the queue in the hangar. Zillah primarily worked on designing all the elements that worked together for the sequence to operate correctly. It wasn't until recently that she left the actual building and programming to other team members. She worked on the box's design and specifications for quite some time, but it didn't seem important until they had more than one ship to operate on missions.

Eirwen followed the specifications that Zillah had created for the queueing system hardware. Most of the system was virtual. The physical parts seemed strangely similar to how the medallion relics attached, but shaped differently. She completed the electronics and connections inside the box, letting the control room team know they could begin integrating the programming with the equipment.

The queue programming was an orchestrated way of closing and opening the portal between drone launches. The queue system would automatically create the proper distance between drones when delivering them to a historical time. Once the three-minute window was up, although it could be cycled sooner, it would move to the next queue setting. The algorithm of Earth's trajectory was already programmed into the software. They typically needed to change only the coordinates and altitude around the Earth's nucleus. They extended and configured the programming parameters to include Earth's historical and near future paths. The intricate part of programming would deliver the drones adjacent to one another in various patterns once they came through the portal. Most of the time, the flying patterns were triangles, unless more drones were present that could design other patterns with more points.

It took a few weeks for the crew to fine-tune the queueing system's accuracy. When Zillah followed up with everyone, she learned everything was progressing as they had planned. However, she still decided to inspect various pieces of the code to ensure they wouldn't have any issues. She knew Eirwen was a perfectionist and would follow her diagrams, so there was no need to shadow her on every move. Still, Zillah also knew that it would be difficult to mess up simple diagram instructions she had designed. Of course, they would eventually test the new system, but some initial checks would give her comfort.

The growing team began to prepare for a mission where all three drones would arrive together in the past, using the new queue system. The next morning, all hands were on deck and at their posts to test the new queueing system that would send multiple crafts back through the portal. They hadn't planned to go back very far in time, this sequence. Still, they wanted to test the drone's maneuverability with the box surrounding it. They launched the first drone that Zillah piloted while the second and third waited to embark.

As the portal opened, she thrust the craft in its large box through the dark fluid. The concept was that when she viewed her console, she should see the other drones on the other side once she had gone through the portal. Even though they hadn't actually launched yet, they would enter the alternate time simultaneously. They planned to go through several maneuvers, then go into long-term storage until the next mission. When she got to the other side, there were no other drones, only hers.

"I don't see the other drones. This can't be a good sign. What's going on?" Zillah questioned with a concerned voice.

"The queue doesn't appear to be cycling," Garret answered quickly.

"Abort the queue! Bogie, bogie, bogie. Looks like a fighter jet," Zillah said frantically, as alarms rang on her display.

The jet was tracking her via radar. She first dropped her hands, entering an assisted free fall to quickly get off the same altitude as the plane. She swung her arms rapidly in several directions to avert from the radars, but it was locked on. She began using several strategies, reiterating that it was foreign technology and far faster than his plane. The drone fell with incredible speed and incomprehensible gravity forces that a human-piloted craft couldn't withstand. After increasing speed to get out of view of the fighter, she finally plunged into the ocean, off the plane's radar. As the box and drone sank into the sea, she took a breath of relief that it was only a brief incident. These encounters were supposed to be planned, not arbitrary.

She powered down the drone and threw her glasses across the desk, clenching her teeth together with frustration.

"Figure it out!" she yelled and stormed out of the room to her office.

After returning to her office, she broke down and cried. She knew she wasn't fair, yelling at the crew, but wondered how much more she could handle on her own. Suddenly, she considered something Jorge wrote to her before passing. She closed her eyes as she remembered the note. *Our paths crossed because they were meant to, and I enjoyed every minute of it. There will be a time soon when we won't be together, but I will see you again someday. Our future and past are intertwined. It's becoming apparent the lines are rapidly becoming blurred. You are a strong and beautiful woman, and you made me a better person because of it. We had our rough spots too, but I will always love you!*

Opening her eyes, she gathered herself once again. Then she decided to apologize to the crew for the sudden outburst and help find the programming issue.

She returned to the control room, where the others were still working on the problems.

"I'm sorry about the outburst. I'm just overly tired, and I got frustrated with the mishap," she began with an apologetic tone.

"Yeah, we're all tired, Zillah! You may be having a difficult time without Jorge, but life goes on, and we have a job to do. I've been the best coworker, leader, and friend I can be, but I can't take much more. You're going to have to come back around. We need you to fill that void that only Jorge could provide. I lost a great friend too, you know," Garret replied hastily with an upset voice.

Ravyn sat awkwardly, quietly, pretending she didn't hear the conversation, but it was loud enough the whole room heard it. Zillah stood for a moment and replied with a simple comment.

"OK."

They sifted through the queue's code the next few days, finding the mistakes that prevented the queue from scrolling to the next time slot. It turned out that it wasn't one mistake but a series of broken logic. After completing the queue, the team powered the portal halfway to recover the drone they left in the ocean. Zillah flew the drone waiting in their current time into the bay for cleaning and additional testing. It was a short, successful mission they had begun to be comfortable with. The team agreed to set the next assignment for the following Monday.

The next Monday was a fairly typical morning for everyone. The team gathered in the conference room to prepare for the events of the day and upcoming missions. Thankfully, the weekend reset everyone's moods and allowed the hostility to be forgotten for the time being.

"The power boxes fared very well during the last trip. From the data I saw, the box lost only a few percent. The drone was full capacity over an approximately three-hundred-year period with one mission. It was a very light load, but I think we can deposit the boxes farther back in time for multiple missions and storage if we lose connection with the drones. I think we've been lucky to this point, considering," Eirwen explained optimistically.

"That's a great point, Eirwen. This would be a good time to leave the boxes and return the drones through the portal. We haven't tested this yet," Garret replied.

"OK, let's plan on sending all three drones through the portal and storing the boxes. We'll use this to test re-entry back to the bay instead of recovery. I also like the idea of putting a 'return to box' code in the drones in case we lose connection with them. Let's work on that, and we'll reschedule the flights in two more days." Zillah concluded the meeting with a half-smile, like they were back on track.

A few days passed, and they were ready to send the drones back through time again. They went through the boot sequence as they usually would. When the

Quarksandrium reached fifty percent power, the UFOd boxes glowed as lights chased each other around the boxes' edges. As the portal reached full power, the portal engaged as it was supposed to and filled the floor with its dark liquid, opening the gateway to the past.

"Here we go," Zillah said with an excited voice.

She motioned her palms upward, and the box lifted off the ground. She hovered the craft above the portal, then dropped through it to the other side. Garret touched some keys to complete the portal cycle, and it immediately closed and reopened. The second box went through, and then the third followed the same sequence.

"We're all here!" Zillah exclaimed with exuberance.

They had all shown up at the same exact second. Although the ships moved together in the past, Zillah was ahead of the rest of the pilots in their own timeline. Yet, they all moved synchronously throughout their mission. Sometimes it was hard to comprehend what was going on. It was part of the mystery of the relics.

"Follow me to the waypoint," Zillah said, moving her craft toward sea level, making the dive into the deep blue.

The other drones followed the same motions in perfect rhythm. It was easier than it appeared, since Zillah gave the crew commands with a little lead time. Each drone pilot had a countdown timer in their heads-up display with the time differential of the crafts, so they could act as one unit. As the three boxes fell through the ocean, they calmly paused and waited for them to fall silently to the bottom.

They had located the boxes in the Pacific Ocean. They weren't far from Hawaii but distant and deep enough that they wouldn't be found. Garret began preparing the portal for the return journey. Suddenly, just as Garret brought the power to one hundred percent, everything went dark. The emergency lights kicked on, and the building was quiet. They had lost control and the connections to the drones. The drones continued hovered for thirty seconds before returning to the boxes waiting for them on the ocean's floor.

"This isn't good," Zillah said with frustration again.

It seemed that fear and anger were always an incident away lately, and everything seemed to digress quickly. Fifteen seconds went by before the generators came on. The power eventually returned about two minutes later.

"That was weird," Garret said, furrowing his brow, then continued with a history lesson. "We have only lost power one other time in the time I've been here."

The crew spent the next day and a half searching for what caused the building's power to go out, but there was no logical explanation. The utility division didn't even notice a power outage. In the days following, Zillah called all the members together for a brief meeting.

"We couldn't find the source of the power outage. It didn't even show up on the records in the utility department. The only possible explanation I can think of is someone turned a breaker off, then back on," Zillah explained, delivering her statements to the crew.

"That's kind of what it seemed like from the bay area too," one of the crew said.

"We need to bring the ships back. Let's plan for tomorrow morning. As you know, there's a comet orbiting the next couple of weeks. Our recovery mission shouldn't affect it, and it shouldn't affect us. We need to be mindful of these events, since we will be entering Earth's atmosphere from space in the near future. Let's keep our eyes open tomorrow and make it a good mission," Zillah said as she gathered her personal items from the conference room table and returned to her office.

The next morning came quickly, with all that needed to be done. As the team planned to bring the drones back, they powered on their computers and instruments for the next flights. It was an optimistic day for the group after the unfortunate events of yesterday. Zillah began by asking Garret to bring the portal up to half power.

"Operational, Captain," Garret said as the Quarksandrium reached fifty percent.

"Initiate flight systems," Zillah commanded.

"Open boxes and prepare to launch," she continued saying to the other flight crew.

"Ready for flight," Gryffen replied.

"Confirmed," Alejandra echoed.

Zillah began rising through the water, with the others following behind. Although they used the queueing system to arrive, when they departed the past, the plan was to use a singular portal opening when they returned to the future. As they approached the ocean's surface, Zillah told Garret to bring the portal to full power.

"Copy," Garret said, then raised the power level of the portal.

When it reached full power, the portal opened. As the three ships exited the ocean, they saw the portal open above the drones. They quickly went through the portal, returning to the bay in their current time. The ships touched down as the three pilots shut the ships down for the next mission. Zillah pulled her glasses off with the heads-up display and breathed a sigh of relief.

"Sequence the portal down. Let's call it a mission," Zillah said.

Garret was reaching to cycle down the portal when the portal abruptly closed.

"What... is going on?" Garret said as he paused before touching the controls.

"What do you mean?" Zillah asked as everyone looked at Garret.

"The portal closed! I didn't do anything. It's still at full power. It shouldn't be at full power with the portal closed. The Quarksandrium should automatically power down to fifty percent if the portal isn't open," he said frantically.

The portal suddenly began to initialize again. The portal opened from the center of the Quarksandrium outward to the edges, as it usually would. However, instead of closing from the portal's outer edge to the center, it closed from the center near the Quarksandrium outward.

"I don't understand what is happening," Garret said in a panic, not knowing what to do. He scoured through the Quarksandrium settings, trying to find out what it was doing.

"Just shut it down!" Zillah exclaimed.

Garret pushed and swiped through screens of information, trying to shut the portal down.

"I'm trying. It's not cooperating," Garret said with frustration.

It continued to stay consistent for the full three minutes. Shortly after, the portal began going through a second sequence. It opened another portal, this time from the outside of the portal inward to the Quarksandrium. It was only momentary, before the portal closed normally. Immediately the equipment went back to half power.

"There we go! We got it back," Garret conveyed in relief. He continued powering down the systems, as his hands still shook from all the nervous energy.

"We need to figure out what happened. Pull the

logs and get them to me ASAP! I don't like the feeling I'm getting from this," Zillah said over the communication devices.

She returned to her office while the crew gathered logs from the equipment to see what exactly just happened. She unlocked her door and continued to sit down at her desk. She was out of sorts and needed a distraction, so she turned on the television for some background noise. She had developed a nervous tic of grabbing the red cloth from the back of her drawer recently with all the stress she was enduring. It was no different today. As she reached for the fabric, her ear caught what the news was saying on the television.

"...a comet in close proximity to the sun disappeared earlier. It is unknown where the comet went at this time. We are waiting for comments from NASA on this development..."

Zillah's eyes got large, and she dropped the cloth she was holding in her hand. She ran next door to the control room and threw the door open.

"Garret, do you have the reports from the return trip yet?" she questioned with urgency.

"Yeah, I just pulled them up. The logs are right here," he said, concerned with where she was going with this frantic questioning. She pushed Garret out of the way and began to search through the logs.

"Right here! What are these coordinates?" she asked frantically.

"I'm not sure. Ravyn, look these coordinates up,

please. I'm sending them…"

"…there's another one," Zillah interrupted.

Ravyn frantically looked up at the two positions and turned in shock to the two.

"The first one is several thousand miles off Earth's orbit."

"What about the second?" Zillah replied.

Ravyn's eyes got even more expansive, and she was scared to even say the results.

"It looks to be between Mars and the Ceres asteroid Belt," Ravyn replied as she turned pale. Zillah turned and looked at Garret.

"Keep searching. See if you can figure out what is going on," she said frantically as she left the control room.

"Got it," Garret replied, nodding as he turned back to his station.

Zillah ran down the hall. She burst through the doors of the bay area and ran to Eirwen.

"Where's the key to the queue box?" she asked her daughter.

"Right here." She reached in her pocket and pulled out a set of keys.

"You are the only one who has a key to that box, correct?" Zillah asked while taking the keys and walking toward the box.

"Yeah, it hasn't been out of my possession," Eirwen said, shocked her mom would insinuate foul play.

Zillah continued walking toward the heart of the

queue system. She found a box that sat near a row of servers in an adjacent room. Long lines of cables went directly from the box to the Quarksandrium. She opened the door to the system. Looking inside, she immediately froze in terror. Right before her eyes was the same wand from the box they took with them to meet Goramaius. The tip and the hilt were between two contact points of the device, as if it had been designed to hold it. Its connections were similar to the medallion relics on the drones and the Quarksandrium orb. Draped over the wand was a red cloth.

"Eirwen!" she screamed, calling her daughter into the next room.

As she entered the room, Eirwen had a confused look on her face.

"What is going on? Why are you freaking out?"

"Did you build it like this?" Zillah questioned, stretching her hand out toward the box.

"What is that?" Eirwen took a closer look and removed the wand's tension, taking it and the cloth out with it.

"I built the rest of the box like that, but these don't belong here," Eirwen said as she held the objects in her hand. Zillah grabbed the two items from her hand and darted out the door.

"What is that? Where are you going?" Eirwen yelled while Zillah ran away.

THE DISCOVERY

Zillah ran back to her office, opening her door in a frantic rush. She nearly locked herself out by moving her hand too quickly on the biometric scanner. The third attempt finally let her through the door. She went behind the desk where she had dropped the red cloth. Zillah picked it up and realized the only other piece like this would have been behind Jorge's memorial plaque, where she pinned it. She began heading for her vehicle, suiting up along the way. The closer she got to her car, the more anxious she became. Her walk became faster until the occasional trot broke through. She couldn't contain the anxiety anymore and started on a full run. When she finally got to the car, she was gasping for breath as she fumbled, trying to open the door. Zillah stood at the door, hunched over for a bit, breathing heavily until she was calmed down enough to get inside. After Zillah got in the car, she drove out of the complex and spoke to the vehicle, entering navigational commands.

"Proceeding to Memorial Park," the car announced.

Once the vehicle assumed command of the controls, Zillah reached for the relic she had put in the cupholder. It was identical. Every last detail engraved down its sides matched the relic in the box that day. She began thinking. *How could this have got into a locked facility with so many security points? If this was the same wand, how did it get from Goramaius back to here?* These relics were more trouble than she thought they would be. Her mind recounted the incidents years ago and danced around all the thoughts of dealing with her projects. Things that happened many years ago suddenly flooded back to her.

Arriving at the memorial site, she went inside, leaving the articles in the vehicle. Flooded with emotion, she didn't know whether to be sad or be angry. Zillah approached the memorial bust of her husband, framed on the wall between many others. When she looked behind the picture, the cloth was gone. *Who, how, why?* She didn't know what to think first.

Any sorrow that was left had changed to anger as she ran back to the car again. This time she prepared the car verbally before even getting to it. The door opened, and as she jumped in and closed the door, it immediately took off toward headquarters as soon as she fastened her belt. The ride in both directions gave her ample time to think and reconsider her actions. Although at this point, it may have been making it more dramatic than it needed to be.

Zillah studied the different pieces in her hands.

The elongated relic and two red cloths. It had never occurred to her when she cut the original piece from Jorge's suit, but after comparing the two... They were identical. How had she not realized this before? The cloth she thought was just random in the Quarksandrium before the trip was the same cloth that she cut from his suit later. It even had the same faded spots and strange burn marks along the edges. *Who brought it back in time? What kind of game was this?*

Returning to her original parking spot, she exited the vehicle. She wondered why things looked so different after an incident like this as she wandered back into the building that she just left an hour earlier. With her head tilted slightly downward, she looked through the top of her eyes down the long hallways with frustration and anger. She passed through the familiar glass-windowed tunnel leading to the main headquarters. It was evident to anyone who encountered her that she was angry and on a mission of vengeance.

When she finally got to the conference room doors, she paused with deep angry breaths and stared at the door. She wasn't even sure if there would be anyone behind the doors. She took a deep breath to calm herself, but the fury arose again as she began pounding on the large doors.

"Let me in! You cowards! How could you have done this?"

Her screams permeated the door as she beat the bottom of her fist against the solid wood doors.

Suddenly she heard a beep, and the doors began opening. Zillah stormed into the room. To her surprise, there were only four beings in the room. They were all wearing red suits with crimson robes and sashes. The rest of the seats were empty. She looked around before raising her voice again.

"Why? Why did you do this?" she questioned in an angry tone. The four members sat quietly for a moment, waiting.

"Well, are you going to say anything?" she asked loudly.

There was another long pause, as she was visibly frustrated. One of the members to the leader's right just shook their head oddly, almost in disbelief at Zillah's actions. Zillah noticed and threw her hands in the air to gesture, *What is wrong with you?* The leader finally spoke in a calm and modulated voice.

"Do you think this scenario has not been foreseen?" the leader questioned in a strong man's voice, as the second being to the right turned their head toward Zillah and began to speak.

"You can't fight the future or the past. What was, and is, and is to come has already happened. You just need to accept that it is unavoidable."

The female voice was also modulated but yet familiar to Zillah. She began to calm her demeanor. It might have been the group's responses, but she was partially confused by what they said. *Where did these people come from, anyway?*

"Did we cause the Quenomoly?" she questioned the individuals in the room.

"That is not your concern right now," the leader replied.

With increasing frustration, Zillah stormed out of the room again. She wasn't sure what she would do now. She had been working toward something she believed in her whole career, only to find that everything was an illusion. The time travel, the board, this company, everything began to take on a new perspective, but it didn't appear to be a good one.

She finally returned to her office. The television was still on and giving opinions about what had happened with the missing comet. She sat down, feeling defeated. Tears of anger and betrayal streamed down her face as she thought of her father. He died from breathing complications in contaminated air caused by the Quenomoly. It finally dawned on her why it was called Quenomoly and not named after the comet that caused the destruction. She was beside herself, knowing the role that she played in the events. *I am so naïve.* She thought to herself, pondering her life's circumstances.

After sulking and thinking for some time, she went home, not speaking to anyone else. When she got home, she went straight to bed. The weight and mental load of all the events through the day had drained her will to continue. She lay for a long time in bed, considering all her mistakes and missteps. If only she'd had more information about what she was doing or questioned when weird things didn't make sense, maybe she could have prevented it.

Zillah drifted to sleep with random angry and "what-if" thoughts in her head. Random images began forming while she slept. She found herself walking down the stairs from the bedroom to the kitchen. She was still groggy and grabbed a coffee cup from the cupboard to make a coffee when she saw Jorge sitting at the table. Everything was still hazy, even though she was trying to wake up. It was strange, she knew it was Jorge, and it sounded like Jorge, but it couldn't be him. He died years ago. She went to the table to confront him and turned his head to see the face she missed so much. While she was still turning his head toward her, his face turned into one of the beings thought to be from another planet. Her eyes opened wide, and she dropped her coffee cup to the ground, shattering into fragments all over the floor. It was almost slow motion as the pieces ricocheted throughout the kitchen.

Zillah jumped backward and began to run. When she reached the stairs, the monster started talking in an unintelligible, modulated voice. She began to scream and ran up the stairs to escape the terror. She made it to the first landing and turned the corner when the creature's arms reached around her waist, preventing her from going any further. The monster that reminded her of Jorge was still at the bottom of the stairs, but his arms had stretched up the stairs.

"You can't escape your future. It has already happened," the monster said.

Zillah began to fight back, climbing the stairs when she finally woke up in her bed, kicking and fighting the covers that were attacking her. She wasn't sure what had happened or what the dream meant. It was a slow realization that it was only a dream.

She made her way down the stairs, an all too familiar scene from her previous night's sleep. Sipping her morning coffee, she occasionally got flashes of the nightmare she just woke up from. Zillah still pondered the recent events and what she could do to reverse them or avenge what the board had done. First, she had to prove somehow that it was the board who staged this event.

Zillah decided to contact an acquaintance she knew from many years ago when she first began her internship with Zander, Dr. Aubrey Lewis. She was a Doctor of Medicine and worked with nanites and other tiny robotics in the medical field. Dr. Lewis didn't work far from Zillah's building. Zillah decided to arrange a meeting with her in a nearby quiet area. Later, Zillah sent her a message requesting to meet her for coffee at one of the complex's vending areas.

Later that morning, Zillah was waiting for Dr. Lewis around the corner from where they were to meet. When she finally arrived, the doctor began to question her about the mysterious meeting arrangement.

"What's going on? Why so secretive? It's been a

while. I hope everything is OK," she inquired, concerned something wasn't quite right.

"I'm OK. A little bit stressed, though," Zillah said as she looked over her shoulder behind her, then quickly got to the point of her conversation.

"Listen, could you do me a favor? I need a bug bot for surveillance. Think you could help?"

"Umm... Yeah, no problem. I'll bring it to your office," Aubrey replied with hesitation.

"No... I'll send you the coordinates of where to drop it. And make it one from your personal inventory. Zander can't find out about this," Zillah insisted as she abruptly completed the meeting.

She touched her hand as she quickly exited the area and continued down the hall as if nothing had happened. The doctor looked confused and worried but continued drinking her coffee while she pulled her phone out to investigate.

When Zillah returned to her office, she sent her friend a message with a location for the drop that would be inconspicuous. Zillah continued and finished her morning routine in her office, thinking it would appear less weird to the others. After completing a few emails, she went to make rounds first in the control room.

"Morning, Ravyn. Where's Garret?" she questioned as she walked through the door.

"I'm not sure. He never came in today," Ravyn replied in a worried and subdued voice.

"He seemed kind of different last night after every-thing happened," Gryffen added from across the room.

Zillah began to think to herself and quietly began calling the contact numbers she had saved in her phone as she walked back to her office. The phone rang until it reached voicemail; there was no answer. Zillah tried the other numbers she had, but it was the same result. It was strange because he was always available. She looked through her email to see if he left any messages or evidence of where he was go-ing. Halfway down the page, there was an email from Garret with the subject *I'm sorry.*

She froze for a minute before she opened the email. *Zillah, I'm really having a difficult time with all of this. Knowing I played a role in facilitating the events that brought the Quenomoly to pass is more than I can handle. I will miss you, my friend. Best Wishes, Garret.* She couldn't believe what she was reading as she be-gan thinking. *He can't be gone. I have to get to his house and bring him back. It wasn't his fault. It had to have been the board.*

It was getting late in the day, and she decided to go find him before he did something terrible or regret-table. Zillah drove across town to his house, entering through the guest parking by the street. As she walked up to the front of the house through the tunnel, the door was cracked open.

"This isn't good. This isn't good at all." Zillah mo-mentarily stopped using her "thinking voice" as the words escaped her mouth. Her heart was beating faster as she gently pushed the door open. Her eyes widened in astonishment. Everything was gone. Garret, his family, the furniture, pictures, everything was gone. There was no food in the refrigerator. Not even the kids' toys that were usually scattered around the living room floor. *How could he just leave so quickly? Where did he go?* There were a lot of questions she still had about everything that was happening. It was all happening so fast, and she could hardly control her emotions.

Since Garret's house was a fruitless lead, she decided to return to work. Shortly after arriving, she received a message from her friend Aubrey that said "*dropped.*" Zillah knew what it meant. She swung by the place where she asked Aubrey to leave the tiny bot. Zillah found a small ring box not far from the coffee shop they met at earlier. It was nestled in the mulch under a tree in the common area. She put it in her pocket and kept walking, in case someone was watching her. It was already early evening, and her crew had gone home for the day.

Back in her office, she cracked the tiny box open to inspect the device. When she opened the box, the tiny intricate robot that she requested was looking back at her with large bug eyes. It was a close resemblance to a horsefly.

"It's perfect." She logged into her computer and synced the device.

The bot would need only a simple flight path programmed in it. Zillah's plan was to traverse the abysmal gateway and fly to a nearby doorway. She programmed simple objectives for the bot and the visual angles she needed. Closing the box, she locked her office and went to the control room.

Zillah began powering on the equipment. The monitors and computers went through a normal boot sequence. As they were initiating and coming online, she grabbed the small box and walked to the bay area. She threw the door open and placed the unit out of the way near the portal. When she arrived back in the control room, the equipment was ready for its next steps. It would take a little longer, since it was just her operating the large portal, but it was possible. She didn't need to hold it open for long—only long enough for the bug to fly through.

Once more, the Quarksandrium came online, and all systems changed to green as it became functional. She pushed the power from zero to fifty percent as the center began to glow and gyrate. She only hoped nobody would interrupt the process. Nearly thirty minutes had passed since she started, and the machine was almost to full power. Just then, the portal opened and committed to the time she had programmed. Quickly, she initiated the sequence, launching the bug through the hole to the other side. As the bug crossed the plane, she began shutting everything down. It was up to a tiny robot from here on out. It would hold all the answers she needed.

As she shut the equipment down, Zillah was careful to remove any logs created, signifying she had opened a portal by herself that wasn't scheduled. After powering down the equipment, she returned everything as if she hadn't been there, and went to the bay area. The great thing about sending objects to the past was that she could instantly recover what she sent back. She walked quickly to the bay area to retrieve the box and the tiny surveillance bug. Putting the bug back in the box, she returned to her office. It seemed simple enough, but had it worked?

After logging into her computer, she opened the file folders containing the footage from the surveillance bot. The file path she had programmed inside the bug was set to save its recorded data in a hidden folder on her personal drive. It was a simple program that contained her credentials to write to a specific folder on the servers. Everything needed to capture images and save them to the network storage was programmed into that tiny bug.

Zillah began viewing the video logs. It showed Eirwen building the queue box and connecting it to the portal. Various team members came and went throughout the day in the bay area. It all seemed like regular activity. She searched as fast as the frames would allow her to comprehend. She didn't want to miss anything but needed answers quickly. Suddenly she realized she had already passed it when she watched herself open the box, taking the wand and red cloth out. *How could I have missed it?* She passed through the archive three more times before realizing that there was time missing from the video. It was the night between the power outage and the portal incident. *How could hours of video be missing? Zillah's* only thought was one she didn't want to think about. It frightened and enraged her to believe that they watched the team that closely, like an experiment.

Over the next few days, she tried to pass the time and not give any suspicion to the rest of her crew, but it wasn't easy. Zillah used the missions as a distraction. Even though she missed Jorge and Garret, she still continued on. After adding in a few seemingly ordinary missions, she wanted to see exactly what happened. She configured the machine with the parameters of the most recent Quenomoly. She set the time for 2333, just before the incident. The distance was a nominal distance, but close enough that they could see what happened. They knew the exact time it happened, so they could return through the same portal without creating a second portal opening.

Zillah wondered what had happened or if viewing this would be a mistake, but she continued anyway. She felt she needed resolution in order to continue on. Gryffen had moved over to Garret's engineering position, since he was the next most knowledgeable in that area. Ravyn was still commanding the overall control room that had been Jorge's original spot, and Zillah would fly the drone UFOd to examine the incident. As they counted down to engagement, Zillah took a deep breath and looked around. She scanned her eyes around the room to just absorb everything at that moment. Looking down into the bay area, she noticed Eirwen checking settings and preparing for the drone's departure. She had grown so fast; Zillah wished she had spent more time bonding with her rather than wrapped up in work and focused on the past. It was a somber experience, almost like a final journey, even though she didn't know why and had no reason to feel that way.

As the portal opened, Gryffen looked over, waiting for the craft to take off and exit through the portal, but it didn't. He rolled his seat over to Zillah and touched her arm as he noticed her gazing at Eirwen.

"Are you OK?" he questioned with concern.

Zillah jerked a bit from being startled, suddenly aware of her surroundings.

"Uh, yes. Thank you. Right... launching," Zillah continued saying as if nothing happened. She gestured her hands, and the drone lifted and quickly vanished through the portal.

"I sure hope this is the right coordinates and time," she commented.

It wasn't like Zillah to doubt herself, but lately, she realized she wasn't as aware as she initially thought.

"Me too," Ravyn replied with a doubting voice.

Zillah's hands and arms hovered above her desk

as she gazed through her heads-up display glasses at the large monitors delivering the footage of space. She still wasn't entirely back to normal in the moment. It was almost like someone was controlling her arms for her, and she was watching from the sidelines.

Zillah realized she was watching the wrong side of the drone. As she changed the view to the other side of the ship, they could see the comet shooting through the sky, bright, large, and an amazing sight to witness. Suddenly a much more expansive portal appeared. She never noticed that the doorway she had arrived through was gone. The Quenomoly portal was three hundred times larger than any they had created before. Initially, it grew from the middle outward as it stabilized and completed the enormous doorway. It was huge, swallowing the comet just as fast as it had appeared. The three minutes approached quickly. When Zillah turned to exit through her own portal back home, she decided she had seen enough.

"Where is the portal, Gryffen?" she asked forcefully.

"It closed as soon as the other portal opened. I can't get it back open," Gryffen said as he pushed buttons on the console.

"I'm going through," Zillah said at the last minute.

She darted through the portal just before it closed behind her.

"Gryffen, open another portal in twenty thirty-four and get me out of here quick," Zillah said frantically.

"I'm on it. We're up," he said. It should be behind you.

Zillah began maneuvering toward the portal while she watched the comet behind her approach Mars.

"Do you see that?" Zillah asked as she watched behind the drone, steering toward the portal.

"I think so, but to be sure... What are you talking about?" Ravyn asked.

"The comet is missing half its tail. Also, the drone has its own tail when in space. It must be from the propulsion design," Zillah said with amazement.

She moved her hands and arms as the drone returned to the bay, and she gently set it down. Powered off her equipment and sat for a few seconds, speechless as she removed her eyewear and flight rings. The whole experience was as if she saw a movie unfolding in front of her. Almost like the entire sequence didn't even exist.

"I hope they didn't see the drone in the past. They would have been watching the comet closely," Zillah said.

The reality of the situation began to sit in with Zillah again as her thoughts began flooding back. She quietly and lethargically left the control room, dragging her feet across the hall to her office. She plopped down heavily in her office chair behind her desk and broke down in tears again. She couldn't remember the last time she had this much trouble with any situation she had encountered. She had suppressed it for so long.

Even when it occasionally tried to surface, she se-
questered it, pushing it back down into a locked vault.
As anyone knows, a person can only hide feelings for
so long before it begins destruction and rips a person
apart both physically and mentally. It was too much
for her to handle. The loss of her husband, coworker,
and even knowing she played an indirect part in her
dad's death. The people who were lost on the day of
the Quenomoly was too much for her to contain any
longer.

As she retreated into a numbed state of mind, she
left her office in her vehicle, waiting in the company
garage. She programmed in the destination and let it
take her home. As she passed by the familiar buildings, she never really gave them much thought before
today. She even burned each tree in her memory as
the vehicle quickly passed them by. Flashbacks and
intertwined visions of what the world was and what it
could have been entered her mind, continually flashing
back and forth. Memories of viewing past sunsets from
the drone and yet living under a tarnished atmosphere.
It was as if the two sides were tearing her apart.

The vehicle finally approached her house, pulling
into the garage. The doors closed behind, pressuriz-
ing the space and expelling dirty air. An elegant exchange from death to life passed right in front of her
eyes. Zillah breathed an enormous sigh of relief as if
there were a new sun shining ahead. She suddenly felt
relief and realized it was always supposed to be that

way. She had been tormenting herself over something that was not controlled by her. It was just something that happened.

She began to think of the two red squares she had from Jorge's suit. *Maybe I should dye the rest and make something of it as a memorial instead of clenching these little pieces.* She began to think of all thing things she could do to make it a wonderful piece. *Perhaps an old-fashioned quilt, maybe a satchel or bag. Would a scarf be too weird?* She climbed the stairs to her bedroom to retrieve the old suit of Jorge's. Sifting through the clothes, she went through the whole closet. *I thought I left it in here. Maybe I moved it to a different closet*, she vaguely remembered. She went from closet to closet throughout the house. Downstairs, upstairs, it didn't seem to be anywhere.

She couldn't think of any place she would have left it. Then it occurred to her: Eirwen's closet was the only one she hadn't checked. As she stood before the door, she couldn't remember putting it in there, and Eirwen moved out of the house years ago. She opened the door and ran a finger across the dresser, displacing the thick dust as she stepped toward the closet. Her old clothes seemed to pile up in this room since Eirwen got married and moved out. There were dresses and suits mixed together of hers and Jorge's. She pushed the articles of clothing from one side of the closet to the other. A slew of memories flooded her mind as each piece of apparel passed in front of her.

Zillah's eyes widened as she began to see the edge of the suit in the back of the closet, but there seemed to be something else hiding behind it. She took his suit in one hand and reached for the red suit behind it with the other. *It couldn't be...*

She backed out of the closet to see both the suits in a better light. When the light struck the glorious red-colored suit with flowing crimson sashes in all its glory, a needle pierced her skin. She felt the warm sensation travel through her body, and suddenly, she began to feel nauseous. Within a few seconds, her knees buckled underneath her as she fell to the floor. Her eyes were still half-open when she faintly recognized the person who administered the paralytic concoction. She lost consciousness as a group came in, scooping her up on a gurney, shuttling Zillah to an emergency vehicle waiting outside. What was beyond the pain would be a new beginning.